STORIES IN
THE DARK

STORIES IN THE DARK

BARRY PAIN

WILDSIDE PRESS

INTRODUCTION

Barry Eric Odell Pain (1864–1928) was an English humorist, poet, and author. These days he is best remembered for his dark fantasy as well as his parodies and humorous stories.

Pain was educated at Cambridge and became a prominent contributor to *The Granta*. James Payn included his story "The Hundred Gates" in the *Cornhill Magazine* in 1889, and shortly afterward he became a contributor to *Punch* and *The Speaker* and joined the staffs of the *Daily Chronicle* and *Black and White*. From 1896 to 1928 he was a regular contributor to *The Windsor Magazine*.

A review of his 1914 collection *Stories Without Tears* in *The Independent* raves about his work:

> Not since Mr. Leonard Merrick's stories, *Whispers About Women*, were first published in this country has imported fiction offered the brilliance and charm of Barry Pain's Stories Without Tears. Like Mr. Merrick, Pain has had to achieve great success in England before being introduced to the American public. While Kipling was writing his *The Light That Failed* and *Barrack Room Ballads*. Pain was doing his first work; like Kipling, he, too, owes his discovery to Robert Louis Stevenson, who compared him to De Maupassant.
>
> Barry Pain is another of the modern Action writers who have gone to school to Dickens for their methods of observation. Beneath the foibles and the satire of provincial life one feels instinctively the brush-strokes that created the Todgers and the Pecksniffs, but set down with a crispness of expression altogether modern. The especial welcome of these tales, some comic, some witty, others pathetic or tragic, however, is in their great simplicity. Ably they refute that rising cult which does excessive reverence to the "technique" of the

short story, forgetful of the fact that the greatest art lies neither in "situations" nor "climax," but in a luminous insight into human character served by a sympathetic and painstaking hand.

Pain died in Bushey, in Hertfordshire and is buried in Bushey churchyard.

If you enjoy *Stories in the Dark*, check out his other collection, *Stories in Gray* (1911), which contains more notable dark fantasies. Scanning his bibliography, I note several books with intriguing titles that may have fantastic content, including *The New Gulliver and Other Stories* (1913), *The Shadow of the Unseen* (1907, written with James Blyth), and *An Exchange of Souls* (1911). For now, I will leave them to other researchers to investigate.

—John Betancourt
Cabin John, Maryland

THE GRAY CAT

I heard this story from Archdeacon M——. I should imagine that it would not be very difficult, by trimming it a little and altering the facts here and there, to make it capable of some simple explanation; but I have preferred to tell it as it was told to me.

After all, there is some explanation possible, even if there is not one definite and simple explanation clearly indicated. It must rest with the reader whether he will prefer to believe that some of the so-called uncivilized i-aces may possess occult powers transcending anything of which the so-called civilized are capable, or whether he will consider that a series of coincidences is sufficient to account for the extraordinary incidents which, in a plain brief way, I am about to relate. It does not seem to me essential to state which view I hold myself, or if I hold neither, and have reasons for not stating a third possible explanation.

I must add a word or two with regard to Archdeacon M——. At the time of this story he was in his fiftieth year. He was a fine scholar, a man of considerable learning. His religious views were remarkably broad; his enemies said remarkably thin. In his younger days he had been something of an athlete, but owing to age, sedentary habits, and some amount of self-indulgence, he had grown stout, and no longer took exercise in any form. He had no nervous trouble of any kind. His death, from heart disease, took place about three years ago. He told me the story twice, at my request; there was an interval of about six weeks between the two narrations; some of the details were elicited by questions of my own. With this preliminary note, we may proceed to the story.

* * * *

In January, 1881, Archdeacon M——, who was a great admirer of Tennyson's poetry, came up to London for a few days, chiefly in order to witness the performance of 'The Cup,' at the Lyceum. He was not present on the first night (Monday, January 3), but on a later night in the same week. At that time, of course, the poet had not received his peerage, nor the actor his knighthood.

On leaving the theatre, less satisfied with the play than with the magnificence of the setting, the Archdeacon found some slight difficulty in getting a cab. He walked a little way down the Strand to find one, when he encountered unexpectedly his old friend, Guy Breddon.

Breddon (that was not his real name) was a man of considerable fortune, a member of the learned societies, and devoted to Central African exploration. He was two or three years younger than the archdeacon, and a man of tremendous physique.

Breddon was surprised to find the Archdeacon in London, and the Archdeacon was equally surprised to find Breddon in England at all. Breddon carried off the Archdeacon with him to his rooms, and sent a servant in a cab to the Langham to pay the Archdeacon's bill and fetch his luggage. The Archdeacon protested, but faintly, and Breddon would not hear of his hospitality being refused.

Breddon's rooms were an expensive suite immediately over a ruinous upholsterer's in a street off Berkeley Square. There was a private street-door, and from it a private staircase to the first and second floors.

The suite of rooms on the first floor, occupied by Breddon, was entirely shut off from the staircase by a door. The second floor suite, tenanted by an Irish M. P., was similarly shut off, and at that time was unoccupied.

Breddon and the Archdeacon passed through the street-door and up the stairs to the first landing, from whence, by the staircase-door, they entered the flat. Breddon had only recently taken the flat, and the Archdeacon had never been there before. It consisted of a broad L-shaped passage with rooms opening into it. There were many trophies on the walls. Horned heads glared at them; stealthy but stuffed beasts watched them furtively from under tables. There was a perfect arsenal of murderous weapons gleaming brightly under the shaded gaslights.

Breddon's servant prepared supper for them before leaving for the Langham, and soon the two men were discussing Mr. Tennyson, Mr. Irving, and a parody of the 'Queen of the May' which had recently appeared in *Punch*, and doing justice to some oysters, a cold pheasant with an excellent salad, and a bottle of '74 Pommery. It was characteristic of the Archdeacon that he remembered exactly the items of the supper, and that Breddon rather neglected the wine.

After supper they passed into the library, where a bright fire was burning. The Archdeacon walked towards the fire, rubbing his plump hands together. As he did so, a portion of the great rug of gray fur on which he was standing seemed to rise up. It was a gray cat of enormous size, larger than any that the Archdeacon had ever seen before, and of the same colour as the rug on which it had been sleeping. It rubbed itself affectionately against the Archdeacon's leg, and purred as he bent down to stroke it.

'What an extraordinary animal!' said the Archdeacon. 'I had no idea cats could grow to this size. Its head's queer, too—so much too small for the body.'

'Yes,' said Breddon, 'and his feet are just as much too big.'

The gray cat stretched himself voluptuously under the Archdeacon's caressing hand, and the feet could be seen plainly. They were very broad, and the claws, which shot out, seemed unusually powerful and well developed. The beast's coat was short, thick, and wiry.

'Most extraordinary!' the Archdeacon repeated.

He lowered himself into a comfortable chair by the fire. He was still bending over the cat and playing with it when a slight chink made him look up. Breddon was putting something down on the table behind the liquor decanters.

'Any particular breed?' the Archdeacon asked.

'Not that I know of. Freakish, I should say. We found him on board the boat when I left for home—may have come there after mice. He'd have been thrown overboard but for me. I got rather interested in him. Smoke?'

'Oh, thank you.'

Outside a cold north wind screamed in quick gusts. Within came the sharp scratch of the match on the ribbed glass as the Archdeacon lit his cigar, the bubble of the rose-water in Breddon's hookah, the soft step of Breddon's man carrying the Archdeacon's luggage into the bedroom at the end of the L-shaped passage, and the constant purring of the big gray cat.

'And what's the cat's name?' the Archdeacon asked.

Breddon laughed.

'Well, if you must have the plain truth, he's called Gray Devil—or, more frequently. Devil *tout court*.'

'Really, now, really, you can't expect an Archdeacon to use such abominable language. I shall call him Gray—or perhaps Mr. Gray would be more respectful, seeing the shortness of our acquaintance. Do you object to the smell of smoke, Mr. Gray? The intelligent beast does not object. Probably you've accustomed him to it.'

'Well, seeing what his name is he could hardly object to smoke, could he?'

Breddon's servant entered. As the door opened and shut, one heard for a moment the crackle of the newly-lit fire in the room that awaited the Archdeacon. The servant swept up the hearth, and, under archdeaconal direction, mixed a lengthy brandy-and-soda. He retired with the information that he would not be wanted again that night.

'Did you notice,' asked the Archdeacon, 'the way Mr. Gray followed your man about? I never saw a more affectionate cat.'

'Think so?' said Breddon. 'Watch this time.'

For the first time he approached the gray cat, and stretched out his hand as if to pet him. In an instant the cat seemed to have gone mad. Its claws shot out, its back hooped, its coat bristled, its tail stood erect; it cursed and spat, and its small green eyes glared. But a close observer would have noticed that all the time it watched not only Breddon, but also that object which had chinked as Breddon had put it down behind the decanters.

The Archdeacon lay back in his chair and laughed heartily.

'What funny creatures they are, and never so funny as when they lose their tempers! Really, Mr. Gray, out of respect to my cloth, you might have refrained from swearing like that. Poor Mr. Gray! Poor puss!'

Breddon resumed his seat with a grim smile. The gray cat slowly subsided, and then thrust its head, as though demanding sympathy, into the fat palm of the Archdeacon's dependent hand.

Suddenly the Archdeacon's eye lighted on the object which the cat had been watching, visible now that the servant had displaced the decanters.

'Goodness me!' he exclaimed, 'you've got a revolver there.'

'That is so,' said Breddon.

'Not loaded, I trust?'

'Oh yes, fully loaded.'

'But isn't that very dangerous?'

'Well, no; I'm used to these things, and I'm not careless with them. I should have thought it more dangerous to have introduced Gray Devil to you without it. He's much more powerful than an ordinary cat, and I fancy there's something beside cat in his pedigree. When I bring a stranger to see him I keep the cat covered with the revolver until I see how the land lies. To do the brute justice, he has always been most friendly with everybody except myself. I'm his only antipathy. He'd have gone for me just now but that he's smart enough to be afraid of this.'

He tapped the revolver.

'I see,' said the Archdeacon seriously, 'and can guess how it happened. You scared him one day by firing the revolver for joke; the report frightened him, and he's never forgiven you or forgotten the revolver. Wonderful memory some of these animals have!'

'Yes,' said Breddon, 'but that guess won't do. I have never, intentionally or by chance, given the "Devil" any reason for his enmity. So far as I know he has never heard a firearm, and certainly he has never heard one since I made his acquaintance. Somebody may have scared him before, and I'm inclined to think that somebody did, for there can be no doubt that the brute knows all that a cat need know about a revolver, and that he's scared of it.

'The first time we met was almost in darkness. I'd got some cases that I was particular about, and the captain had said I could go down to look after them. Well, this beast suddenly came out of a lump of black and flew at me. I didn't even recognise that it was a cat, because he's so mighty big. I fetched him a clip on the side of the head that knocked him off, and whipped out my iron. He was away in a streak. He knew. And I've had plenty of proof since that he knows. He'd bite me now if he had the chance, but he understands that he hasn't got the chance. I'm often half inclined to take him on plain—shooting barred—and to feel my own hands breaking his damned neck!'

'Really, old man, really!' said the Archdeacon in perfunctory protest, as he rose and mixed himself another drink.

'Sorry to use strong language, 'but I don't love that cat, you know.'

The Archdeacon expressed his surprise that in that case Breddon did not get rid of the brute.

'You come across him on board ship and he flies at you. You save his life, give him board and lodging, and he still hates you so much that he won't let you touch him, and you are no fonder of him than he is of you. Why don't you part company?'

'As for his board, I've known him to eat anything except his own kill. He goes out hunting every night. I keep him simply and solely because I'm afraid of him. As long as I can keep him I know my nerves are all right. If I let my funk of him make any difference—well, I shouldn't be much good in a Central African forest. At first I had some idea of taming him—and, besides, there was a queer coincidence.'

He rose and opened the window, and Gray Devil slowly slunk up to it. He paused a few moments on the window-sill and then suddenly sprang and vanished.

'What was the coincidence?'

'What do you think of that?'

Breddon handed the Archdeacon a figure of a cat which he had taken from the mantelpiece. It was a little thing about three inches high. In colour, in the small head, enormous feet, and curiously human eyes, it seemed an exact reproduction of Gray Devil.

'A perfect likeness. How did you get it made?'

'I got the likeness before I got the original. A little Jew dealer sold it me the night before I left for England. He thought it was Egyptian, and described it as an idol. Anyhow, it was a niceish piece of jade.'

'I always thought jade was bright green.'

'It may be—or white—or brown. It varies. I don't think there can be any doubt that this little figure is old, though I doubt if it's Egyptian.'

Breddon put it back in its place.

'By the way, that same night the little Jew came to try and buy it back again. He offered me twice what I had given for it. I said he must have found somebody who was pretty keen on it. I asked if it was a collector. The Jew thought not; said it was a coloured gentleman. Well, that finished it. I wasn't going to do anything to oblige a nigger. The Jew pleaded that it was a particularly fine buck-nigger, with mountains of money, who'd been tracking the thing for years, and hinted at all manner of mumbo-jumbo business—to scare me, I suppose. However, I wouldn't listen, and kicked him out. Then came the coincidence. Having bought the likeness, next day I found the living original. Rum, wasn't it?'

At this moment the clock struck, and the Archdeacon recognised with horror that it was very, very much past the time when respectable Archdeacons should be in bed and asleep. He rose and said good-night, observing that he'd like to hear more about it on the morrow.

This was extremely unfortunate, for it will be seen it is just at this part of the story that one wants full details, and on the morrow it became impossible to elicit them.

Before leaving the library Breddon closed the window, and the archdeacon asked how 'Mr. Gray,' as he called him, would get back.

'Very likely he's back already. He's got a special window in the kitchen, made on purpose, just big enough to let him get in and out as he likes.'

'But don't other cats get in, too?'

'No,' said Breddon. 'Other cats avoid Gray Devil.'

The Archdeacon found himself unaccountably nervous when he got to his room. He owned to me that he had to satisfy himself that there was no one concealed under the bed or in the wardrobe. However, he got into bed, and after a little while fell into a deep sleep; his fire was burning brightly, and the room was quite light.

Shortly after four he was awakened by a loud scream. Still sleepy, he did not for the moment locate the sound, thinking that it must have come from the street outside. But almost immediately afterward he heard the report of a revolver fired twice in quick succession, and then, after a short pause, a third time.

The Archdeacon was terribly frightened. He did not know what had happened, and thought of armed burglars. For a time— he did not think it could have been more than a minute—fear held him motionless. Then with an effort he rose, lit the gas, and hurried on his clothes. As he was dressing, he heard a step down the passage and a knock at his door.

He opened it, and found Breddon's servant. The man had put on a blue overcoat over his night-things, and wore slippers. He was shivering with cold and terror.

'Oh, my God, sir!' he exclaimed, 'Mr. Breddon's shot himself. Would you come, sir?'

The Archdeacon followed the man to Breddon's bedroom. The smoke still hung thickly in the room. A mirror had been smashed, and lay in fragments on the floor. On the bed, with his back to the archdeacon, lay Breddon, dead. His right hand still grasped the revolver, and there was a blackened wound behind the right ear.

When the Archdeacon came round to look at the face he turned faint, and the servant took him out into the library and gave him brandy, the glasses and decanters still standing there. Breddon's face certainly had looked very ghastly; it had been scratched, torn and bitten; one eye was gone, and the whole face was covered with blood.

'Do you think it was that brute did it?'

'Sure of it, sir; sprang on his face while he was asleep. I knew it would happen one of these nights. He knew it too; always slept with the revolver by his side. He fired twice at the brute, but couldn't see for the blood. Then he killed himself."

It seemed likely enough, with his eyesight gone, horribly mauled, in an agony of pain, possibly believing that he was saving himself from a death still more horrible, Breddon might very well have turned the weapon on himself.

'What do we do now?' the man asked.

'We must get a doctor and fetch the police at once. Come on.'

As they turned the corner of the passage, they saw that the door communicating with the staircase was open.

'Did you open that door?' asked the Archdeacon.

'No,' said the man, aghast.

'Then who did?'

'Don't know, sir. Looks as if we weren't at the end of this yet.'

They passed down the stairs together, and found the street-door also ajar. On the pavement outside lay a policeman slowly recovering consciousness. Breddon's man took the policeman's whistle and blew it. A passing hansom, going back to the mews, slowed up; the cab was sent to fetch a doctor, and communication with the police-station rapidly followed.

The injured policeman told a curious story. He was passing the house when he heard shots fired. Almost immediately afterward he heard the bolts of the front-door being drawn, and stepped back into the neighbouring doorway. The front-door opened, and a negro emerged clad in a gray tweed suit with a gray overcoat. The policeman jumped out, and without a second's hesitation the black man felled him. 'It was all done before you could think,' was the policeman's phrase.

'What kind of negro?' asked the Archdeacon.

'A big man—stood over six foot, and black as coal. He never waited to be challenged; the moment he knew that he was seen he hit out.'

The policeman was not a very intelligent fellow, and there was little more to be got out of him. He had heard the shots, seen the street-door open and the man in gray appear, and had been felled by a lightning blow before he had time to do anything.

The doctor, a plain, matter-of-fact little man, had no hesitation in saying that Breddon was dead, and must have died almost immediately. After the injuries received, respiration and heart-action must have ceased at once. He was explaining something which oozed from the dead man's ear, when the Archdeacon could stand it no longer, and staggered out into the library. There he found Breddon's servant, still in the blue overcoat, explaining to a policeman with a notebook that as far as he knew nothing was missing except a jade image or idol of a cat which formerly stood on the mantelpiece.

The cat known as 'Gray Devil' was also missing, and, although a description of it was circulated in the public press, nothing was ever heard of it again. But gray fur was found in the clenched left hand of the dead man.

The inquest resulted in the customary verdict, and brought to light no new facts. But it may be as well to give what the police theory of the case was. According to the police the suicide took place much as Breddon's servant had supposed. Mad with pain and unable to bear the thought of his awful mutilation, Breddon had shot himself.

The story of the jade image, as far as it was known, was told at the inquest. The police held that this image was an idol, that some uncivilized tribe was much perturbed by the theft of it, and was ready to pay an enormously high price for its recovery. The negro was assumed to be aware of this, and to have determined to obtain possession of the idol by fair means or foul. Fair means failing, it was suggested that the negro followed Breddon to England, tracked him out, and on the night in question found some means to conceal himself in Breddon's flat. There it was assumed that he fell asleep, was awakened by the screams and the sound of the firing, and, being scared, caught up the jade image and made off. Realizing that the shots would have been heard outside, and that his departure at that moment would be considered extremely suspicious, he was ready as he opened the street-door to fell the first man that he saw. The temporary unconsciousness of the policeman gave him time to get away.

The theory sounds at first sight like the only possible theory. When the Archdeacon first told me the story, I tried to find out indirectly whether he accepted it. Finding him rather disposed to fence with my hints and suggestions, I put the question to him plainly and bluntly:

'Do you believe in the police theory?'

He hesitated, and then answered with complete frankness:

'No, most emphatically not.'

'Why?' I asked; and he went over the evidence with me.

'In the first place, I do not believe that Breddon, in the ordinary sense, committed suicide. No amount of physical pain would have made him even think of it. He had unending pluck. He would have taken the facial disfigurement and loss of sight as the chances of war, and would have done the best that could be done by a man with such awful disabilities. One must admit that he fired the fatal shot—the medical evidence on that point is too strong to be gainsaid—but he fired it under circumstances of supernatural horror of which we, thank God! know nothing.'

'I'm naturally slow to admit supernatural explanation.'

'Well, let's go on. What's this mysterious tribe the police talk about? I want to know where it lives and what its name is. It's wealthy enough to offer a huge reward; it must be of some importance. The negro managed to get in and secrete himself. How? Where? I know the flat, and that theory won't do. We don't even know that it was the negro who took that little image, though I believe it was. Anyhow, how did the negro get away at that hour of the morning absolutely unobserved? Negroes are not so common in London that they can walk about without being noticed; yet not one trace of him was ever found, and equally mysterious is the disappearance of the Gray Cat. It was such an extraordinary brute, and the description of it was so widely circulated that it would have seemed almost certain we should hear of it again. Well, we've not heard.'

We discussed the police theory for some little time, and something which he happened to say led me to exclaim:

'Really! Do you mean to say that the Gray Cat actually was the negro?'

'No,' he replied, 'not exactly that, but something near it. Cats are strange animals, anyhow, needn't remind you of their connection with certain old religions or with that witchcraft in which even in England today some still believe, and not so long ago almost all believed. I have never, by the way, seen a good explanation of the fact that there are people who cannot bear to be in a room with a cat, and are aware of its presence as if by some mysterious extra sense. Let me remind you of the belief which undoubtedly exists both in China and Japan, that evil spirits may enter into certain of the lower animals, the fox and badger especially. Every student of demonology knows about these things.

'But that idea of evil spirits taking possession of cats or foxes is surely a heathen superstition which you cannot hold.'

'Well, I have read of the evil spirits that entered into the swine. Think it over, and keep an open mind.'

THE UNDYING THING

I

Up and down the oak-panelled dining-hall of Mansteth the master of the house walked restlessly. At formal intervals down the long severe table were placed four silver candlesticks, but the light from these did not serve to illuminate the whole of the surroundings. It just touched the portrait of a fair-haired boy with a sad and wistful expression that hung at one end of the room; it sparkled on the lid of a silver tankard. As Sir Edric passed to and fro it lit up his face and figure. It was a bold and resolute face with a firm chin and passionate, dominant eyes. A bad past was written in the lines of it. And yet every now and then there came over it a strange look of very anxious gentleness that gave it some resemblance to the portrait of the fair-haired boy. Sir Edric paused a moment before the portrait and surveyed it carefully, his strong brown hands locked behind him, his gigantic shoulders thrust a little forward.

'Ah, what I was!' he murmured to himself—'what I was!'

Once more he commenced pacing up and down. The candles, mirrored in the polished wood of the table, had burnt low. For hours Sir Edric had been waiting, listening intently for some sound from the room above or from the broad staircase outside. There had been sounds—the wailing of a woman, a quick abrupt voice, the moving of rapid feet. But for the last hour he had heard nothing. Quite suddenly he stopped and dropped on his knees against the table:

'God, I have never thought of Thee. Thou knowest that—Thou knowest that by my devihsh behaviour and cruelty I did veritably murder Alice, my first wife, albeit the physicians did maintain that she died of a decline—a wasting sickness. Thou knowest that all here in Mansteth do hate me, and that rightly. They say, too, that I am mad; but that they say not rightly, seeing that I know how wicked I am. I always knew it, but I never cared until I loved—oh, God, I never cared!'

His fierce eyes opened for a minute, glared round the room, and closed again tightly. He went on:

'God, for myself I ask nothing; I make no bargaining with Thee. Whatsoever punishment Thou givest me to bear I will bear it; whatsoever Thou givest me to do I will do it. Whether Thou killest Eve or whether Thou keepest her in life—and never have I loved but her—I will from this night be good. In due penitence will I receive the holy Sacrament of Thy Body and Blood. And my son, the one child that I had by Alice, I will fetch back again from Challonsea, where I kept him in order that I might not look upon him, and I will be to him a father in deed and very truth. And in all things, so far as in me lieth, I will make restitution and atonement. Whether Thou hearest me or whether Thou hearest me not, these things shall be. And for my prayer, it is but this: of Thy loving kindness, most merciful God, be Thou with Eve and make her happy; and after these great pains and perils of childbirth send her Thy peace. Of Thy loving-kindness. Thy merciful loving-kindness, O God!'

Perhaps the prayer that is offered when the time for praying is over is more terribly pathetic than any other. Yet one might hesitate to say that this prayer was unanswered.

Sir Edric rose to his feet. Once more he paced the room. There was a strange simplicity about him, the simplicity that scorns an incongruity. He felt that his lips and throat were parched and dry. He lifted the heavy silver tankard from the table and raised the lid; there was still a good draught of mulled wine in it with the burnt toast, cut heart-shape, floating on the top.

'To the health of Eve and her child,' he said aloud, and drained it to the last drop.

Click, click! As he put the tankard down he heard distinctly two doors opened and shut quickly, one after the other. And then slowly down the stairs came a hesitating step. Sir Edric could bear the suspense no longer. He opened the dining-room door, and the dim light strayed out into the dark hall beyond.

'Dennison,' he said, in a low, sharp whisper, 'is that you?'

'Yes, yes. I am coming, Sir Edric.'

A moment afterwards Dr. Dennison entered the room. He was very pale; perspiration streamed from his forehead; his cravat was disarranged. He was an old man, thin, with the air of proud humility. Sir Edric watched him narrowly.

'Then she is dead,' he said, with a quiet that Dr. Dennison had not expected.

'Twenty physicians—a hundred physicians could not have saved her. Sir Edric. She was—' He gave some details of medical interest.

'Dennison,' said Sir Edric, still speaking with calm and restraint, 'why do you seem thus indisposed and panic-stricken? You are a physician; have you never looked upon the face of death before? The soul of my wife is with God—'

'Yes,' murmured Dennison, 'a good woman, a perfect, saintly woman.'

'And,' Sir Edric went on, raising his eyes to the ceiling as though he could see through it, 'her body lies in great dignity and beauty upon the bed, and there is no horror in it. Why are you afraid?'

'I do not fear death, Sir Edric.'

'But your hands—they are not steady. You are evidently overcome. Does the child live?'

'Yes, it lives.'

'Another boy—a brother for young Edric, the child that Alice bore me?'

'There—there is something wrong. I do not know what to do. I want you to come upstairs. And, Sir Edric, I must tell you, you will need your self-command.'

'Dennison, the hand of God is heavy upon me; but from this time forth until the day of my death I am submissive to it, and God send that that day may come quickly! I will follow you and I will endure.'

He took one of the high silver candlesticks from the table and stepped towards the door. He strode quickly up the staircase. Dr. Dennison following a little way behind him.

As Sir Edric waited at the top of the staircase he heard suddenly from the room before him a low cry. He put down the candlestick on the floor and leaned back against the wall listening. The cry came again, a vibrating monotone ending in a growl.

'Dennison, Dennison!'

His voice choked; he could not go on.

'Yes,' said the doctor, 'it is in there. I had the two women out of the room, and got it here. No one but myself has seen it. But you must see it, too.'

He raised the candle and the two men entered the room— one of the spare bedrooms. On the bed there was something moving under cover of a blanket. Dr. Dennison paused for a moment and then flung the blanket partially back.

They did not remain in the room for more than a few seconds. The moment they got outside, Dr. Dennison began to speak.

'Sir Edric, I would fain suggest somewhat to you. There is no evil, as Sophocles hath it in his "Antigone," for which man hath not found a remedy, except it be death, and here—'

Sir Edric interrupted him in a husky voice.

'Downstairs, Dennison. This is too near.'

It was, indeed, passing strange. When once the novelty of this—this occurrence had worn off. Dr. Dennison seemed no longer frightened. He was calm, academic, interested in an unusual phenomenon. But Sir Edric, who was said in the village to fear nothing in earth, or heaven, or hell, was obviously much moved.

When they had got back to the dining-room. Sir Edric motioned the doctor to a seat.

'Now, then,' he said, 'I will hear you. Something must be done—and to-night.'

'Exceptional cases,' said Dr. Dennison, 'demand exceptional remedies. Well, it lies there up-stairs and is at our mercy. We can let it live, or, placing one hand over the mouth and nostrils, we can—'

'Stop,' said Sir Edric. 'This thing has so crushed and humiliated me that I can scarcely think. But I recall that while I waited for you I fell upon my knees and prayed that God would save Eve. And, as I confessed unto Him more than I will ever confess unto man, it seemed to me that it were ignoble to offer a price for His favour. And I said that whatsoever punishment I had to bear, I would bear it; and whatsoever He called upon me to do, I would do it; and I made no conditions.'

'Well?'

'Now my punishment is of two kinds. Firstly, my wife. Eve, is dead. And this I bear more easily because I know that now she is numbered with the company of God's saints, and with them her pure spirit finds happier communion than with me; I was not worthy of her. And yet she would call my roughness by gentle, pretty names. She gloried, Dennison, in the mere strength of my body, and in the greatness of my stature. And I am thankful that she never saw this—this shame that has come upon the house. For she was a proud woman, with all her gentleness, even as I was proud and bad until it pleased God this night to break me even to the dust. And for my second punishment, that, too, I must bear. This thing that lies upstairs, I will take and rear; it is bone of my bone and flesh of my flesh; only, if it be possible, I will hide my shame so that no man but you shall know of it.'

'This is not possible. You cannot keep a living being in this house unless it be known. Will not these women say, "Where is the child?"'

Sir Edric stood upright, his powerful hands linked before him, his face working in agony; but he was still resolute.

'Then if it must be known, it shall be known. The fault is mine. If I had but done sooner what Eve asked, this would not have happened. I will bear it.'

'Sir Edric, do not be angry with me, for if I did not say this, then I should be but an ill counsellor. And, firstly, do not use the word shame. The ways of nature are past all explaining; if a woman be frail and easily impressed, and other circumstances concur, then in some few rare cases a thing of this sort does happen. If there be shame, it is not upon you but upon nature—to whom one would not lightly impute shame. Yet it is true that common and uninformed people might think that this shame was yours. And herein lies the great trouble—the shame would rest also on her memory.'

'Then,' said Sir Edric, in a low, unfaltering voice, 'this night for the sake of Eve I will break my word, and lose my own soul eternally.'

About an hour afterwards Sir Edric and Dr. Dennison left the house together. The doctor carried a stable lantern in his hand. Sir Edric bore in his arms something wrapped in a blanket. They went through the long garden, out into the orchard that skirts the north side of the park, and then across a field to a small dark plantation known as Hal's Planting. In the very heart of Hal's Planting there are some curious caves: access to the innermost chamber of them is exceedingly difficult and dangerous, and only possible to a climber of exceptional skill and courage. As they returned from these caves. Sir Edric no longer carried his burden. The dawn was breaking and the birds began to sing.

'Could not they be quiet just for this morning?' said Sir Edric wearily.

There were but few people who were asked to attend the funeral of Lady Vanquerest and of the baby which, it was said, had only survived her by a few hours. There were but three people who knew that only one body—the body of Lady Van-querest—was really interred on that occasion. These three were Sir Edric Vanquerest, Dr. Dennison, and a nurse whom it had been found expedient to take into their confidence.

During the next six years Sir Edric lived, almost in solitude, a life of great sanctity, devoting much of his time to the education of the younger Edric, the child that he had by his first wife. In the course of this time some strange stories began to be told and believed in the neighbourhood with reference to Hal's Planting, and the place was generally avoided.

When Sir Edric lay on his death-bed the windows of the chamber were open, and suddenly through them came a low cry. The doctor in attendance hardly regarded it, supposing that it came from one of the owls in the trees outside. But Sir Edric, at the sound of it, rose right up in bed before anyone could stay him, and flinging up his arms cried, 'Wolves! wolves! wolves!' Then he fell forward on his face, dead.

And four generations passed away.

II

Towards the latter end of the nineteenth century, John Marsh, who was the oldest man in the village of Mansteth, could be prevailed upon to state what he recollected. His two sons supported him in his old age; he never felt the pinch of poverty, and he always had money in his pocket; but it was a settled principle with him that he would not pay for the pint of beer which he drank occasionally in the parlour of The Stag. Sometimes Farmer Wynthwaite paid for the beer; sometimes it was Mr. Spicer from the post-office; sometimes the landlord of The Stag himself would finance the old man's evening dissipation. In return, John Marsh was prevailed upon to state what he recollected; this he would do with great heartiness and strict impartiality, recalling the intemperance of a former Wynthwaite and the dishonesty of some ancestral Spicer while he drank the beer of their direct descendants. He would tell you, with two tough old fingers crooked round the handle of the pewter that you had provided, how your grandfather was a poor thing, 'fit for nowt but to brak steeans by ta rord-side.' He was so disrespectful that it was believed that he spoke truth. He was particularly disrespectful when he spoke of that most devilish family, the Vanquerests; and he never tired of recounting the stories that from generation to generation had grown up about them. It would be objected, sometimes, that the present Sir Edric, the last surviving member of the race, was a pleasant-spoken young man, with none of the family wildness and hot temper. It was for no sin of his that Hal's Planting was haunted—a thing which everyone in Mansteth, and many beyond it, most devoutly believed. John Marsh would hear no apology for him, nor for any of his ancestors; he recounted the prophecy that an old mad woman had made of the family before her strange death, and hoped, fervently, that he might live to see it fulfilled.

The third baronet, as has already been told, had lived the latter part of his life, after his second wife's death, in peace and quietness. Of him John Marsh remembered nothing, of course, and could only recall the few fragments of information that had been handed down to him. He had been told that this Sir Edric, who had travelled a good deal, at one time kept wolves, intending to train them to serve as dogs; these wolves were not kept under proper restraint, and became a kind of terror to the neighbourhood. Lady Vanquerest, his second wife, had asked him frequently to destroy these beasts; but Sir Edric, although it was said that he loved his second wife even more than he hated the first, was obstinate when any of his whims were crossed, and put her off with promises. Then one day Lady Vanquerest herself was attacked by the wolves; she was not bitten, but she was badly frightened. That filled Sir Edric with remorse, and, when it was too late, he went out into the yard where the wolves were kept and shot them all. A few months afterwards Lady Vanquerest died in childbirth. It was a queer things John Marsh noted, that it was just at this time that Hal's Planting began to get such a bad name. The fourth baronet was, John Marsh considered, the worst of the race; it was to him that the old mad woman had made her prophecy, an incident that Marsh himself had witnessed in his childhood and still vividly remembered.

The baronet, in his old age, had been cast up by his vices on the shores of melancholy; heavy-eyed, gray-haired, bent, he seemed to pass through life as in a dream. Every day he would go out on horseback, always at a walking pace, as though he were following the funeral of his past self. One night he was riding up the village street as this old woman came down it. Her name was Ann Ruthers; she had a kind of reputation in the village, and although all said that she was mad, many of her utterances were remembered, and she was treated with respect. It was growing dark, and the village street was almost empty; but just at the lower end was the usual group of men by the door of The Stag, dimly illuminated by the light that came through the quaint windows of the old inn. They glanced at Sir Edric as he rode slowly past them, taking no notice of their respectful salutes. At the upper end of the street there were two persons. One was Ann Ruthers, a tall, gaunt old woman, her head wrapped in a shawl; the other was John Marsh. He was then a boy of eight, and he was feeling somewhat frightened. He had been on an expedition to a distant and fœtid pond, and in the black mud and clay about its borders he had discovered live newts; he had three of them in his pocket, and this was to some extent a joy to him, but his joy was damped by his knowledge that he was coming home much too late, and would probably be chastised in consequence. He was unable to walk fast or to run, because Ann Ruthers was immediately in front of him, and he dared not pass her, especially at night. She walked on until she met Sir Edric, and then, standing still, she called him by name. He pulled in his horse and raised his heavy eyes to look at her. Then in loud clear tones she spoke to him, and John Marsh heard and remembered every word that she said; it was her prophecy of the end of the Vanquerests. Sir Edric never answered a word.

When she had finished, he rode on, while she remained standing there, her eyes fixed on the stars above her. John Marsh dared not pass the mad woman; he turned round and walked back, keeping close to Sir Edric's horse. Quite suddenly, without a word of warning, as if in a moment of ungovernable irritation, Sir Edric wheeled his horse round and struck the boy across the face with his switch.

On the following morning John Marsh—or rather, his parents—received a handsome solatium in coin of the realm; but sixty-five years afterwards he had not forgiven that blow, and still spoke of the Vanquerests as a most devilish family, still hoped and prayed that he might see the prophecy fulfilled. He would relate, too, the death of Ann Ruthers, which occurred either later on the night of her prophecy or early on the following day. She would often roam about the country all night, and on this particular night she left the main road to wander over the Vanquerest lands, where trespassers, especially at night, were not welcomed. But no one saw her, and it seemed that she had made her way to a part where no one was likely to see her; for none of the keepers would have entered Hal's Planting by night. Her body was found there at noon on the following day, lying under the tall bracken, dead, but without any mark of violence upon it. It was considered that she had died in a fit. This naturally added to the ill-repute of Hal's Planting. The woman's death caused considerable sensation in the village. Sir Edric sent a messenger to the married sister with whom she had lived, saying that he wished to pay all the funeral expenses. This offer, as John Marsh recalled with satisfaction, was refused.

Of the last two baronets he had but little to tell. The fifth baronet was credited with the family temper, but he conducted himself in a perfectly conventional way, and did not seem in the least to belong to romance. He was a good man of business, and devoted himself to making up, as far as he could, for the very extravagant expenditure of his predecessors. His son, the present Sir Edric, was a fine young fellow and popular in the village.

Even John Marsh could find nothing to say against him; other people in the village were interested in him. It was said that he had chosen a wife in London—a Miss Guerdon—and would shortly be back to see that Mansteth Hall was put in proper order for her before his marriage at the close of the season. Modernity kills ghostly romance. It was difficult to associate this modern and handsome Sir Edric, bright and spirited, a good sportsman and a good fellow, with the doom that had been foretold for the Vanquerest family. He himself knew the tradition and laughed at it. He wore clothes made by a London tailor, looked healthy, smiled cheerfully, and, in a vain attempt to shame his own head-keeper, had himself spent a night alone in Hal's Planting. This last was used by Mr. Spicer in argument, who would ask John Marsh what he made of it. John Marsh replied, contemptuously, that it was 'nowt.' It was not so that the Vanquerest family was to end; but when the thing, whatever it was, that lived in Hal's Planting, left it and came up to the house, to Mansteth Hall itself, then one would see the end of the Vanquerests. So Ann Ruthers had prophesied. Sometimes Mr. Spicer would ask the pertinent question, how did John Marsh know that there really was anything in Hal's Planting? This he asked, less because he disbelieved, than because he wished to draw forth an account of John's personal experiences. These were given in great detail, but they did not amount to very much. One night John Marsh had been taken by business—Sir Edric's keepers would have called the business by hard names—into the neighbourhood of Hal's Planting. He had there been suddenly startled by a cry, and had run away as though he were running for his life. That was all he could tell about the cry—it was the kind of cry to make a man lose his head and run. And then it always happened that John Marsh was urged by his companions to enter Hal's Planting himself, and discover what was there. John pursed his thin lips together, and hinted that that also might be done one of these days. Whereupon Mr. Spicer looked across his pipe to Farmer Wynthwaite, and smiled significantly.

Shortly before Sir Edric's return from London, the attention of Mansteth was once more directed to Hal's Planting, but not by any supernatural occurrence. Quite suddenly, on a calm day, two trees there fell with a crash; there were caves in the centre of the plantation, and it seemed as if the roof of some big chamber in these caves had given way.

They talked it over one night in the parlour of The Stag. There was water in these caves. Farmer Wynthwaite knew it; and he expected a further subsidence. If the whole thing collapsed, what then?

'Ay,' said John Marsh. He rose from his chair, and pointed in the direction of the Hall with his thumb. 'What then?'

He walked across to the fire, looked at it meditatively for a moment, and then spat in it.

'A trewly wun'ful owd mon,' said Farmer Wynthwaite as he watched him.

III

In the smoking-room at Mansteth Hall sat Sir Edric with his friend and intended brother-in-law, Dr. Andrew Guerdon. Both men were on the verge of middle-age; there was hardly a year's difference between them. Yet Guerdon looked much the older man; that was, perhaps, because he wore a short, black beard, while Sir Edric was clean-shaven. Guerdon was thought to be an enviable man. His father had made a fortune in the firm of Guerdon, Guerdon and Bird; the old style was still retained at the bank, although there was no longer a Guerdon in the firm. Andrew Guerdon had a handsome allowance from his father, and had also inherited money through his mother. He had taken the degree of Doctor of Medicine; he did not practise, but he was still interested in science, especially in out-of-the-way science. He was unmarried, gifted with perpetually good health, interested in life, popular. His friendship with Sir Edric dated from their college days. It had for some years been almost certain that Sir Edric would marry his friend's sister, Ray Guerdon, although the actual betrothal had only been announced that season.

On a bureau in one corner of the room were spread a couple of plans and various slips of paper. Sir Edric was wrinkling his brows over them, dropping cigar-ash over them, and finally getting angry over them. He pushed back his chair irritably, and turned towards Guerdon.

'Look here, old man!' he said. I desire to curse the original architect of this house—to curse him in his down-sitting and his uprising.'

'Seeing that the original architect has gone to where beyond these voices there is peace, he won't be offended. Neither shall I. But why worry yourself? You've been rooted to that blessed bureau all day, and now, after dinner, when every self-respecting man chucks business, you return to it again—even as a sow returns to her wallowing in the mire.'

'Now, my good Andrew, do be reasonable. How on earth can I bring Ray to such a place as this? And it's built with such ingrained malice and vexatiousness that one can't live in it as it is, and can't alter it without having the whole shanty tumble down about one's ears. Look at this plan now. That thing's what they're pleased to call a morning room. If the window had been *here* there would have been an uninterrupted view of open country. So what does this forsaken fool of an architect do? He sticks it *there*, where you see it on the plan, looking straight on to a blank wall with a stable yard on the other side of it. But that's a trifle. Look here again—'

'I won't look any more. This place is all right. It was good enough for your father and mother and several generations before them until you arose to improve the world; it was good enough for you until you started to get married. It's a picturesque place, and if you begin to alter it you'll spoil it.' Guerdon looked round the room critically. 'Upon my word,' he said, 'I don't know of any house where I like the smoking-room as well as I like this. It's not too big, and yet it's fairly lofty; it's got those comfortable-looking oak-panelled walls. That's the right kind of fireplace, too, and these corner cupboards are handy.'

'Of course this won't *remain* the smoking-room. It has the morning sun, and Ray likes that, so I shall make it into her boudoir. It *is* a nice room, as you say.'

'That's it, Ted, my boy,' said Guerdon bitterly; 'take a room which is designed by nature and art to be a smoking-room and turn it into a boudoir. Turn it into the very deuce of a boudoir with the morning sun laid on for ever and ever. Waste the twelfth of August by getting married on it. Spend the winter in foreign parts, and write letters that you can breakfast out of doors, just as if you'd created the mildness of the climate yourself. Come back in the spring and spend the London season in the country in order to avoid seeing anybody who wants to see you. That's the way to do it; that's the way to get yourself generally loved and admired!'

'That's chiefly imagination,' said Sir Edric. 'I'm blest if I can see why I should not make this house fit for Ray to live in.'

'It's a queer thing: Ray was a good girl, and you weren't a bad sort yourself. You prepare to go into partnership, and you both straightway turn into despicable lunatics. I'll have a word or two with Ray. But I'm serious about this house. Don't go tinkering it; it's got a character of its own, and you'd better leave it. Turn half Tottenham Court Road and the culture thereof— Heaven help it!—into your town house if you like, but leave this alone.'

'Haven't got a town house—yet. Anyway I'm not going to be unsuitable; I'm not going to feel myself at the mercy of a big firm. I shall supervise the whole thing myself. I shall drive over to Challonsea tomorrow afternoon and see if I can't find some intelligent and fairly conscientious workmen.'

'That's all right; you supervise them and I'll supervise you. You'll be much too new if I don't look after you. You've got an old legend, I believe, that the family's coming to a bad end; you must be consistent with it. As you are bad, be beautiful. By the way, what do you yourself think of the legend?'

'It's nothing,' said Sir Edric, speaking, however, rather seriously. 'They say that Hal's Planting is haunted by something that will not die. Certainly an old woman, who for some godless reason of her own made her way there by night, was found there dead on the following morning; but her death could be, and was, accounted for by natural causes. Certainly, too, I haven't a man in my employ who'll go there by night now.'

'Why not?'

'How should I know? I fancy that a few of the villagers sit boozing at The Stag in the evening, and like to scare themselves by swopping lies about Hal's Planting. I've done my best to stop it. I once, as you know, took a rug, a revolver and a flask of whiskey and spent the night there myself. But even that didn't convince them.'

'Yes, you told me. By the way, did you hear or see anything?'

Sir Edric hesitated before he answered. Finally he said:

'Look here, old man, I wouldn't tell this to anyone but yourself I did think that I heard something. About the middle of the night I was awakened by a cry; I can only say that it was the kind of cry that frightened me. I sat up, and at that moment I heard some great, heavy thing go swishing through the bracken behind me at a great rate. Then all was still; I looked about, but I could find nothing. At last I argued as I would argue now that a man who is just awake is only half awake, and that his powers of observation, by hearing or any other sense, are not to be trusted. I even persuaded myself to go to sleep again, and there was no more disturbance. However, there's a real danger there now. In the heart of the plantation there are some eaves and a subterranean spring; lately there has been some slight subsidence there, and the same sort of thing will happen again in all probability. I wired today to an expert to come and look at the place; he has replied that he will come on Monday. The legend says that when the thing that lives in Hal's Planting comes up to the Hall the Vanquerests will be ended. If I cut down the trees and then break up the place with a charge of dynamite I shouldn't wonder if I spoiled that legend.'

Guerdon smiled.

'I'm inclined to agree with you all through. It's absurd to trust the immediate impressions of a man just awakened; what you heard was probably a stray cow.'

'No cow,' said Sir Edric impartially. 'There's a low wall all round the place—not much of a wall, but too much for a cow.'

'Well, something else—some equally obvious explanation. In dealing with such questions, never forget that you're in the nineteenth century. By the way, your man's coming on Monday. That reminds me to-day's Friday, and as an indisputable consequence to-morrow's Saturday, therefore, if you want to find your intelligent workmen it will be of no use to go in the afternoon.'

'True,' said Sir Edric, 'I'll go in the morning.' He walked to a tray on a side table and poured a little whiskey into a tumbler. 'They don't seem to have brought any seltzer water,' he remarked in a grumbling voice.

He rang the bell impatiently.

'Now why don't you use those corner cupboards for that kind of thing? If you kept a supply there, it would be handy in case of accidents.'

'They're full up already.'

He opened one of them and showed that it was filled with old account-books and yellow documents tied up in bundles. The servant entered.

'Oh, I say, there isn't any seltzer. Bring it, please.'

He turned again to Guerdon.

'You might do me a favour when I'm away to-morrow, if there's nothing else that you want to do. I wish you'd look through all these papers for me. They're all old. Possibly some of them ought to go to my solicitor, and I know that a lot of

them ought to be destroyed. Some few may be of family interest. It's not the kind of thing that I could ask a stranger or a
servant to do for me, and I've so much on hand just now before
my marriage—'

'But of course, my dear fellow, I'll do it with pleasure.'

'I'm ashamed to give you all this bother. However, you said
that you were coming here to help me, and I take you at your
word. By the way, I think you'd better not say anything to Ray
about the Hal's Planting story.'

'I may be some of the things that you take me for, but really
I am not a common ass. Of course I shouldn't tell her.'

'I'll tell her myself, and I'd sooner do it when I've got the
whole thing cleared up. Well, I'm really obliged to you.'

'I needn't remind you that I hope to receive as much again.
I believe in compensation. Nature always gives it and always
requires it. One finds it everywhere, in philology and onwards.'

'I could mention omissions.'

'They are few, and make a belief in a hereafter to supply
them logical.'

'Lunatics, for instance?'

'Their delusions are often their compensation. They argue
correctly from false premises. A lunatic believing himself to be
a millionaire has as much delight as money can give.'

'How about deformities or monstrosities?'

'The principle is there, although I don't pretend that the
compensation is always adequate. A man who is deprived of one
sense generally has another developed with unusual acuteness.
As for monstrosities of at all a human type one sees none; the
things exhibited in fairs are, almost without exception, frauds.
They occur rarely, and one does not know enough about them.
A really good text-book on the subject would be interesting.
Still, such stories as I have heard would bear out my theory—
stories of their superhuman strength and cunning, and of the
extraordinary prolongation of life that has been noted, or is said
to have been noted, in them. But it is hardly fair to test my prin-

ciple by exceptional cases. Besides, anyone can prove anything except that anything's worth proving.'

'That's a cheerful thing to say. I wouldn't like to swear that I could prove how the Hal's Planting legend started; but I fancy, do you know, that I could make a very good shot at it.'

'Well?'

'My great-grandfather kept wolves—I can't say why. Do you remember the portrait of him?—not the one when he was a boy, the other. It hangs on the staircase. There's now a group of wolves in one corner of the picture. I was looking carefully at the picture one day and thought that I detected some over-painting in that corner; indeed, it was done so roughly that a child would have noticed it if the picture had been hung in a better light. I had the over-painting removed by a good man, and underneath there was that group of wolves depicted. Well, one of these wolves must have escaped, got into Hal's Planting, and scared an old woman or two; that would start a story, and human mendacity would do the rest.'

'Yes,' said Guerdon meditatively, 'that doesn't sound improbable. But why did your great-grandfather have the wolves painted out?'

IV

Saturday morning was fine, but very hot and sultry. After breakfast, when Sir Edric had driven off to Challonsea, Andrew Guerdon settled himself in a comfortable chair in the smoking-room. The contents of the corner cupboard were piled up on a table by his side. He lit his pipe and began to go through the papers and put them in order. He had been at work about a quarter of an hour when the butler entered rather abruptly, looking pale and disturbed.

'In Sir Edric's absence, sir, it was thought that I had better come to you for advice. There's been an awful thing happened.'

'Well?'

'They've found a corpse in Hal's Planting about half an hour ago. It's the body of an old man, John Marsh, who used to live in the village. He seems to have died in some kind of a fit. They were bringing it here, but I had it taken down to the village where his cottage is. Then I sent to the police and to a doctor.'

There was a moment or two's silence before Guerdon answered.

'This is a terrible thing. I don't know of anything else that you could do. Stop; if the police want to see the spot where the body was found, I think that Sir Edric would like them to have every facility.'

'Quite so, sir.'

'And no one else must be allowed there.'

'No, sir. Thank you.'

The butler withdrew.

Guerdon arose from his chair and began to pace up and down the room.

'What an impressive thing a coincidence is!' he thought to himself. 'Last night the whole of the Hal's Planting story seemed to me not worth consideration. But this second death there—it can be only coincidence. What else could it be?'

The question would not leave him. What else could it be? Had that dead man seen something there and died in sheer terror of it? Had Sir Edric really heard something when he spent that night there alone? He returned to his work, but he found that he got on with it but slowly. Every now and then his mind wandered back to the subject of Hal's Planting. His doubts annoyed him. It was unscientific and unmodern of him to feel any perplexity, because a natural and rational explanation was possible; he was annoyed with himself for being perplexed.

After luncheon he strolled round the grounds and smoked a cigar. He noticed that a thick bank of dark, slate-coloured clouds was gathering in the west. The air was very still. In a remote corner of the garden a big heap of weeds was burning; the smoke went up perfectly straight. On the top of the heap light flames danced; they were like the ghosts of flames in the strange light. A few big drops of rain fell. The small shower did not last for five seconds. Guerdon glanced at his watch. Sir Edric would be back in an hour, and he wanted to finish his work with the papers before Sir Edric's return, so he went back into the house once more.

He picked up the first document that came to hand. As he did so, another, smaller, and written on parchment, which had been folded in with it, dropped out. He began to read the parchment; it was written in faded ink, and the parchment itself was yellow and in many places stained. It was the confession of the third baronet—he could tell that by the date upon it. It told the story of that night when he and Dr. Dennison went together carrying a burden through the long garden out into the orchard that skirts the north side of the park, and then across a field to a small, dark plantation. It told how he made a vow to God and did not keep it. These were the last words of the confession:

'Already upon me has the punishment fallen, and the devil's wolves do seem to hunt me in my sleep nightly. But I know that there is worse to come. The thing that I took to Hal's Planting is dead. Yet will it come back again to the Hall, and then will the Vanquerests be at an end. This writing I have committed to chance, neither showing it nor hiding it, and leaving it to chance if any man shall read it.'

Underneath there was a line written in darker ink, and in quite a different handwriting. It was dated fifteen years later, and the initials R.D. were appended to it:

'It is not dead. I do not think that it will ever die.'

When Andrew Guerdon had finished reading this document, he looked slowly round the room. The subject had got on his nerves, and he was almost expecting to see something. Then he did his best to pull himself together. The first question he put to himself was this: 'Has Ted ever seen this? Obviously he had not. If he had, he could not have taken the tradition of Hal's Planting so lightly, nor have spoken of it so freely. Besides, he would either have mentioned the document to Guerdon, or he would have kept it carefully concealed. He would not have allowed him to come across it casually in that way. 'Ted must never see it,' thought Guerdon to himself. He then remembered the pile of weeds he had seen burning in the garden. He put the parchment in his pocket, and hurried out. There was no one about. He spread the parchment on the top of the pile, and waited until it was entirely consumed. Then he went back to the smoking-room; he felt easier now.

'Yes,' thought Guerdon, 'if Ted had first of all heard of the finding of that body, and then had read that document, I believe that he would have gone mad. Things that come near us affect us deeply.'

Guerdon himself was much moved. He clung steadily to reason; he felt himself able to give a natural explanation all through, and yet he was nervous. The net of coincidence had closed in around him; the mention in Sir Edric's confession of the prophecy which had subsequently become traditional in the village alarmed him. And what did that last line mean? He supposed that R.D. must be the initials of Dr. Dennison. What did he mean by saying that the thing was not dead? Did he mean that it had not really been killed, that it had been gifted with some preternatural strength and vitality and had survived, though Sir Edric did not know it? He recalled what he had said about the prolongation of the lives of such things. If it still survived, why had it never been seen? Had it joined to the wild hardiness of the beast a cunning that was human—or more than human? How could it have lived? There was water in the caves, he reflected, and food could have been secured—a wild beast's food. Or did Dr. Dennison mean that though the thing itself was dead, its wraith survived and haunted the place? He wondered how the doctor had found Sir Edric's confession, and why he had written that hue at the end of it. As he sat thinking, a low rumble of thunder in the distance startled him. He felt a touch of panic—a sudden impulse to leave Mansteth at once and, if possible, to take Ted with him. Ray could never live there. He went over the whole thing in his mind again and again, at one time calm and argumentative about it, and at another shaken by blind horror.

Sir Edric, on his return from Challonsea a few minutes afterward, came straight to the smoking-room where Guerdon was. He looked tired and depressed. He began to speak at once:

'You needn't tell me about it—about John Marsh. I heard about it in the village.'

'Did you? It's a painful occurrence, although, of course—'

'Stop. Don't go into it. Anything can be explained—I know that'

'I went through those papers and account-books while you were away. Most of them may just as well be destroyed; but there are a few—I put them aside there—which might be kept. There was nothing of any interest.'

'Thanks; I'm much obliged to you.'

'Oh, and look here, I've got an idea. I've been examining the plans of the house, and I'm coming round to your opinion. There are some alterations which should be made, and yet I'm afraid that they'd make the place look patched and renovated. It wouldn't be a bad thing to know what Ray thought about it.'

'That's impossible. The workmen come on Monday, and we can't consult her before then. Besides, I have a general notion what she would like.'

'We could catch the night express to town at Challonsea, and—'

Sir Edric rose from his seat angrily and hit the table.

'Good God! don't sit there hunting up excuses to cover my cowardice, and making it easy for me to bolt. What do you suppose the villagers would say, and what would my own servants say, if I ran away to-night? I am a coward—I know it. I'm horribly afraid. But I'm not going to act like a coward if I can help it.'

'Now, my dear chap, don't excite yourself. If you are going to care at all—to care as much as the conventional damn—for what people say, you'll have no peace in life. And I don't believe you're afraid. What are you afraid of?'

Sir Edric paced once or twice up and down the room, and then sat down again before replying.

'Look here, Andrew, I'll make a clean breast of it. I've always laughed at the tradition; I forced myself, as it seemed at least, to disprove it by spending a night in Hal's Planting; I took the pains even to make a theory which would account for its origin. All the time I had a sneaking, stifled belief in it. With the help of my reason I crushed that; but now my reason has thrown up the job, and I'm afraid. I'm afraid of the Undying Thing that is in Hal's Planting. I heard it that night. John Marsh saw it last night—they took me to see the body, and the face was awful; and I believe that one day it will come from Hal's Planting—'

'Yes,' interrupted Guerdon, 'I know. And at present I believe as much. Last night we laughed at the whole thing, and we shall live to laugh at it again, and be ashamed of ourselves for a couple of superstitious old women. I fancy that beliefs are affected by weather—there's thunder in the air.'

'No,' said Sir Edric, 'my belief has come to stay.'

'And what are you going to do?'

'I'm going to test it. On Monday I can begin to get to work, and then I'll blow up Hal's Planting with dynamite. After that we shan't need to believe—we shall *know*. And now let's dismiss the subject. Come down into the billiard-room and have a game. Until Monday I won't think of the thing again.'

Long before dinner. Sir Edric's depression seemed to have completely vanished. At dinner he was boisterous and amused. Afterward he told stories and was interesting.

* * * *

It was late at night; the terrific storm that was raging outside had awoke Guerdon from sleep. Hopeless of getting to sleep again, he had arisen and dressed, and now sat in the window-seat watching the storm. He had never seen anything like it before; and every now and then the sky seemed to be torn across as if by hands of white fire. Suddenly he heard a tap at his door, and looked round. Sir Edric had already entered; he also had dressed. He spoke in a curious, subdued voice.

'I thought you wouldn't be able to sleep through this. Do you remember that I shut and fastened the dining-room window?'

'Yes, I remember it.'

'Well, come in here.'

Sir Edric led the way to his room, which was immediately over the dining-room. By leaning out of window they could see that the dining-room window was open wide.

'Burglar,' said Guerdon meditatively.

'No,' Sir Edric answered, still speaking in a hushed voice. 'It is the Undying Thing—it has come for me.'

He snatched up the candle, and made towards the staircase; Guerdon caught up the loaded revolver which always lay on the table beside Sir Edric's bed and followed him. Both men ran down the staircase as though there were not another moment to lose. Sir Edric rushed at the dining-room door, opened it a little, and looked in. Then he turned to Guerdon, who was just behind him.

'Go back to your room,' he said authoritatively.

'I won't,' said Guerdon. 'Why? What is it?'

Suddenly the corners of Sir Edric's mouth shot outward into the hideous grin of terror.

'It's there! It's there!' he gasped.

'Then I come in with you.'

'Go back!'

With a sudden movement, Sir Edric thrust Guerdon away from the door, and then, quick as light, darted in, and locked the door behind him.

Guerdon bent down and listened. He heard Sir Edric say in a firm voice:

'Who are you? What are you?'

Then followed a heavy, snorting breathing, a low, vibrating growl, an awful cry, a scuffle.

Then Guerdon flung himself at the door. He kicked at the lock, but it would not give way. At last he fired his revolver at it. Then he managed to force his way into the room. It was perfectly empty. Overhead he could hear footsteps; the noise had awakened the servants; they were standing, tremulous, on the upper landing.

Through the open window access to the garden was easy. Guerdon did not wait to get help; and in all probability none of the servants could have been persuaded to come with him. He climbed out alone, and, as if by some blind impulse, started to run as hard as he could in the direction of Hal's Planting. He knew that Sir Edric would be found there.

But when he got within a hundred yards of the plantation, he stopped. There had been a great flash of lightning, and he saw that it had struck one of the trees. Flames darted about the plantation as the dry bracken caught. Suddenly, in the light of another flash, he saw the whole of the trees fling their heads upwards; then came a deafening crash, and the ground slipped under him, and he was flung forward on his face. The plantation had collapsed, fallen through into the caves beneath it. Guerdon slowly regained his feet; he was surprised to find that he was unhurt. He walked on a few steps, and then fell again; this time he had fainted away.

THE END OF A SHOW

It was a little village in the extreme north of Yorkshire, three miles from a railway-station on a small branch line. It was not a progressive village; it just kept still and respected itself The hills lay all round it, and seemed to shut it out from the rest of the world. Yet folks were born, and lived, and died, much as in the more important centres; and there were intervals which required to be filled with amusement. Entertainments were given by amateurs from time to time in the schoolroom; sometimes hand-bell ringers or a conjurer would visit the place, but their reception was not always encouraging. 'Conjurers is nowt, an' ringers is nowt,' said the sad native judiciously; 'ar dornt regard 'em.' But the native brightened up when in the summer months a few caravans found their way to a piece of waste land adjoining the churchyard. They formed the village fair, and for two days they were a popular resort. But it was understood that the fair had not the glories of old days; it had dwindled. Most things in connection with this village dwindled.

The first day of the fair was drawing to a close. It was half-past ten at night, and at eleven the fair would close until the following morning. This last half-hour was fruitful in business. The steam roundabout was crowded, the proprietor of the peep-show was taking pennies very fast, although not so fast as the proprietor of another, somewhat repulsive, show. A fair number patronized a canvas booth which bore the following inscription:

POPULAR SCIENCE LECTURES.
Admission Free.

At one end of this tent was a table covered with red baize; on it were bottles and boxes, a human skull, a retort, a large book, and some bundles of dried herbs. Behind it was the lecturer, an old man, gray and thin, wearing a bright-coloured dressing-gown. He lectured volubly and enthusiastically; his energy and the atmosphere of the tent made him very hot, and occasionally he mopped his forehead.

'I am about to exhibit to you,' he said, speaking clearly and correctly, 'a secret known to few, and believed to have come originally from those wise men of the East referred to in Holy Writ.' Here he filled two test-tubes with water, and placed some bluish-green crystals in one and some yellow crystals in the other. He went on talking, quoting scraps of Latin, telling stories, making local and personal allusions, finally coming back again to his two test-tubes, both of which now contained almost colourless solutions. He poured them both together into a flat glass vessel, and the mixture at once turned to a deep brownish purple. He threw a fragment of something on to the surface of the mixture, and that fragment at once caught fire. This favourite trick succeeded; the audience were undoubtedly impressed, and before they quite realized by what logical connection the old man had arrived at the subject, he was talking to them about the abdomen. He seemed to know the most unspeakable and intimate things about the abdomen. He had made pills which suited its peculiar needs, which he could and would sell in boxes at sixpence and one shilling, according to size. He sold four boxes at once, and was back in his classical and anecdotal stage, when a woman pressed forward. She was a very poor woman. Could she have a box of these pills at half-price? Her son was bad, very bad. It would be a kindness.

He interrupted her in a dry, distinct voice:

'Woman, I never yet did anyone a kindness, not even myself.'

However, a friend pushed some money into her hand, and she bought two boxes.

* * * *

It was past twelve o'clock now. The flaring lights were out in the little group of caravans on the waste ground. The tired proprietors of the shows were asleep. The gravestones in the churchyard were glimmering white in the bright moonlight. But at the entrance to that little canvas booth the quack doctor sat on one of his boxes, smoking a clay pipe. He had taken off the dressing-gown, and was in his shirt-sleeves; his clothes were black, much worn. His attention was arrested—he thought that he heard the sound of sobbing.

'It's a God-forsaken world,' he said aloud. After a second's silence he spoke again. 'No, I never did a kindness even to my-self, though I thought I did, or I shouldn't have come to this.'

He took his pipe from his mouth and spat. Once more he heard that strange wailing sound; this time he arose, and walked in the direction of it.

Yes, that was it. It came from that caravan standing alone where the trees made a dark spot. The caravan was gaudily painted, and there were steps from the door to the ground. He remembered having noticed it once during the day. It was evi-dent that someone inside was in trouble—great trouble. The old man knocked gently at the door.

'Who's there? What's the matter?'

'Nothing,' said a broken voice from within.

'Are you a woman?'

There was a fearful laugh.

'Neither man nor woman—a show.'

'What do you mean?'

'Go round to the side, and you'll see.'

The old man went round, and by the light of two wax match-es caught a glimpse of part of the rough painting on the side of the caravan. The matches dropped from his hand. He came back, and sat down on the steps of the caravan.

'You are not like that,' he said.

'No, worse. I'm not dressed in pretty clothes, and lying on a crimson velvet couch. I'm half naked, in a corner of this cursed box, and crying because my owner beat me. Now go, or I'll open the door and show myself to you as I am now. It would frighten you; it would haunt your sleep.'

'Nothing frightens me. I was a fool once, but I have never been frightened. What right has this owner over you?'

'He is my father,' the voice screamed loudly; then there was more weeping; then it spoke again: 'It's awful; I could bear anything now—anything—if I thought it would ever be any better; but it won't. My mind's a woman's and my wants are a woman's, but I am not a woman. I am a show. The brutes stand round me, talk to me, touch me!'

'There's a way out,' said the old man quietly, after a pause. An idea had occurred to him.

'I know—and I daren't take it—I've got a thing here, but I daren't use it.'

'You could drink something—something that wouldn't hurt?'

'Yes.'

'You are quite alone?'

'Yes; my owner is in the village, at the inn.'

'Then wait a minute.'

The old man hastened back to the canvas booth, and fumbled about with his chemicals. He murmured something about doing someone a kindness at last. Then he returned to the caravan with a glass of colourless liquid in his hand.

'Open the door and take it,' he said.

The door was opened a very little way. A thin hand was thrust out and took the glass eagerly. The door closed, and the voice spoke again.

'It will be easy?'

'Yes.'

'Good-bye, then. To your health—'

The old man heard the glass crash on the wooden floor, then he went back to his seat in front of the booth, and carefully lit another pipe.

'I will not go," he said aloud. 'I fear nothing—not even the results of my best action.'

He listened attentively.

No sound whatever came from the caravan. All was still. Far away the sky was growing lighter with the dawn of a fine summer day.

THE BOTTOM OF THE GULF

Three hundred and sixty-two years before Christ a chasm opened in the Roman Forum, and the soothsayers declared that it would never close until the most precious treasure of Rome had been thrown into it. It is said that a youth named Mettus (or Mettius) Curtius appeared on horseback in full armour, and before a very fair audience, exclaiming that Rome had no dearer possession than arms and courage, leaped down into the gulf, which thereupon closed over him. This incident, like most of the legendary history of Rome, has been subjected to severe criticism. Those who too hastily disbelieve in it will reconsider their opinion on reading the account, not previously published, of what took place at the bottom of the gulf.

Curtius and the horse fell in the order in which they had started, with the horse underneath. After a few minutes' rapid passage the horse stopped falling somewhat suddenly, broke most of itself, and died. Curtius, who, though a little shaken, was uninjured, sat up on his dead horse and looked round to see if he could discover the nearest way back. As he looked upward he saw the top edges of the cavern close together, and the daylight shut out. But a curious greenish light still lingered in the cavern in which he found himself, and from one of its recesses came a voice which startled Mettus considerably. It said interrogatively:

'Did you hurt yourself?'

'Not much,' replied Curtius. 'I didn't know there was anybody down here. You quite startled me. Do come out and let me see you.'

'No, thanks,' said the voice. 'Did you really believe that you would die when you jumped down the gulf?'

'Certainly I did.'

The voice laughed, a mean little snigger.

'So you will, too. You'll die of suffocation, slowly, when the air in this cavern is exhausted.'

'Then we'd better get to work at once,' said Curtius. 'I have an excellent sword here and a couple of daggers. I put them on for the occasion. I didn't fall so far as I expected, and if we both of us work hard we shall be able to cut our way out.'

'Thanks,' said the voice, 'but I'm not going to do any work. I'm not of the same kind as yourself. I don't need the air of the outer world. In fact, I don't think much of the outer world, even its best specimens. That's why I live down here. You've got to die. Sorry, but there's no help for it. I've set my trap, and I caught you, and if you're the best specimen they can provide on top, my low opinion of them is confirmed.'

'What do you mean by the "trap"?' asked Curtius.

'Well, it was I who caused the chasm to open, knowing the kind of tomfool thing your soothsayers would remark about it. I sat here wondering what I should get. Shouldn't have been sur-prised at a brace of vestal virgins. They would have exclaimed, "Purity and devotion," instead of "Courage and arms," amid loud applause, of course. Or it might have been an elderly ma-tron, with a good old tag that Rome held nothing more precious than the tender love of her mothers. It might have been a sooth-sayer, it might have been anything. As it is, it's you, and I think very little of you. Arms? Of what use do you think all those tin-pot arrangements which you have hung about you are likely to be? Courage? Why, man alive! you've got no courage at all.'

'I have,' said Curtius stolidly; 'I fully expected to die, and I was willing to die.'

'Just for one moment,' said the voice, 'when you had got all that mob of howling fools around applauding you. Applause is an intoxicant, and you got drunk on it. Now you are sober again, and you don't want to die at all. The man who can die alone, slowly and terribly, is courageous. But you've got no more courage in you than a piece of chewed string. You're as white as chalk.'

'That's the effect of the green light,' interposed Curtius.

'Rubbish!' replied the voice, 'green light doesn't make a man shake all over, does it?'

'That's just the shock from the fall,' said Curtius. 'But I can't stop here arguing with you; I'm off to explore the cavern. There must be a way out somewhere.'

'There isn't,' said the voice; 'but you can explore.'

'I can't die like a rat in a trap,' said Curtius, whimpering.

And off he went on his exploration. He looked in at the recess from which the voice had proceeded and found nothing. The cave was enormous. For many hours he tramped on and on, and never through one tiny chink in the roof did he see the light of day. Exhausted and ravenous, at last he flung himself down on the floor of the cave, and almost immediately the voice, which had been silent all this time, began again. First of all came that faint, mean little snigger; then it said:

'Hungry?'

'Worn out with hunger,' sobbed Curtius; 'I'm thirsty, too. My mouth is so parched that I can hardly speak, and there doesn't seem to be one drop of moisture in this damned cavern.'

'There isn't,' said the voice, 'nor one crumb of food either, with the exception of your horse, and I don't think you will be able to find that again. You can try back if you like. Now I come to think of it, you won't die of suffocation, but of starvation. Cuts my entertainment rather shorter than I had hoped, but I must put up with that.'

'I can't die like this,' sobbed Curtius.

'Courage and arms,' replied the voice, 'are the things which Rome holds most precious. Go on, my boy; you'll last some time yet.'

Then Curtius drew his sword, and went to look for the proprietor of the voice in order to slay him. But he didn't find him. He resumed his explorations.

In a few hours he was too weak to walk any further. He fell into a kind of doze, and when he woke again his arms had been taken from him.

'Where is my sword?' he exclaimed.

'I've got it,' replied the voice, this time from the roof of the cavern; 'what do you want it for?'

'Want to kill myself,'said Curtius.

'If I give you your sword, will you own that you were merely a drunken theatrical impostor?'

'Yes.'

'And that you are a coward, and are dying the death of a coward?'

'Yes.'

The sword clattered down from the roof on to the floor of the cavern at the feet of the hero.

He picked it up and set his teeth.

THE CASE OF VINCENT PYRWHIT

The death of Vincent Pyrwhit, J. P., of Ellerdon House, Ellerdon, in the county of Buckingham, would in the ordinary way have received no more attention than the death of any other simple country gentleman. The circumstances of his death, however, though now long since forgotten, were sensational, and attracted some notice at the time. It was one of those cases which is easily forgotten within a year, except just in the locality where it occurred. The most sensational circumstances of the case never came before the public at all. I give them here simply and plainly. The psychical people may make what they like of them.

Pyrwhit himself was a very ordinary country gentleman, a good fellow, but in no way brilliant. He was devoted to his wife, who was some fifteen years younger than himself, and remarkably beautiful. She was quite a good woman, but she had her faults. She was fond of admiration, and she was an abominable flirt. She misled men very cleverly, and was then sincerely angry with them for having been misled. Her husband never troubled his head about these flirtations, being assured quite rightly that she was a good woman. He was not jealous; she, on the other hand, was possessed of a jealousy amounting almost to insanity. This might have caused trouble if he had ever provided her with the slightest basis on which her jealousy could work, but he never did. With the exception of his wife, women bored him. I believe she did once or twice try to make a scene for some preposterous reason which was no reason at all; but nothing serious came of it, and there was never a real quarrel between them.

On the death of his wife, after a prolonged illness, Pyrwhit wrote and asked me to come down to Ellerdon for the funeral, and to remain at least a few days with him. He would be quite alone, and I was his oldest friend. I hate attending funerals, but I *was* his oldest friend, and I was, moreover, a distant relation of his wife. I had no choice and I went down.

There were many visitors in the house for the funeral, which took place in the village churchyard, but they left immediately afterwards. The air of heavy gloom which had hung over the house seemed to lift a little. The servants (servants are always very emotional) continued to break down at intervals, noticeably Pyrwhit's man, Williams, but Pyrwhit himself was self-possessed. He spoke of his wife with great affection and regret, but still he could speak of her and not unsteadily. At dinner he also spoke of one or two other subjects, of politics and of his duties as a magistrate, and of course he made the requisite fuss about his gratitude to me for coming down to Ellerdon at that time. After dinner we sat in the library, a room well and expensively furnished, but without the least attempt at taste. There were a few oil paintings on the walls, a presentation portrait of himself, and a landscape or two—all more or less bad, as far as I remember. He had eaten next to nothing at dinner, but he had drunk a good deal; the wine, however, did not seem to have the least effect upon him. I had got the conversation definitely off the subject of his wife when I made a blunder. I noticed an Erichsen's extension standing on his writing-table. I said:

'I didn't know that telephones had penetrated into the villages yet.'

'Yes,' he said, 'I believe they are common enough now. I had that one fitted up during my wife's illness to communicate with her bedroom on the floor above us on the other side of the house.'

At that moment the bell of the telephone rang sharply.

We both looked at each other. I said with the stupid affectation of calmness one always puts on when one is a little bit frightened:

'Probably a servant in that room wishes to speak to you.'

He got up, walked over to the machine, and swung the green cord towards me. The end of it was loose.

'I had it disconnected this morning,' he said; 'also the door of that room is locked, and no one can possibly be in it.'

He had turned the colour of gray blotting-paper; so probably had I. The bell rang again—a prolonged, rattling ring.

'Are you going to answer it?' I said.

'I am not,' he answered firmly.

'Then,' I said, 'I shall answer it myself. It is some stupid trick, a joke not in the best of taste, for which you will probably have to sack one or other of your domestics.'

'My servants,' he answered, 'would not have done that. Besides, don't you see it is impossible? The instrument is disconnected.'

'The bell rang all the same. I shall try it.'

I picked up the receiver.

'Are you there?' I called.

The voice which answered me was unmistakably the rather high staccato voice of Mrs. Pyrwhit.

'I want you,' it said, 'to tell my husband that he will be with me to-morrow.'

I still listened. Nothing more was said.

I repeated, 'Are you there?' and still there was no answer.

I turned to Pyrwhit.

'There is no one there,' I said. 'Possibly there is thunder in the air affecting the bell in some mysterious way. There must be some simple explanation, and I'll find it all out to-morrow.'

* * * *

He went to bed early that night. All the following day I was with him. We rode together, and I expected an accident every minute, but none happened. All the evening I expected him to turn suddenly faint and ill, but that also did not happen. When at about ten o'clock he excused himself and said good-night I felt distinctly relieved. He went up to his room and rang for Williams.

The rest is, of course, well known. The servant's reason had broken down, possibly the immediate cause being the death of Mrs. Pyrwhit. On entering his master's room, without the least hesitation, he raised a loaded revolver which he carried in his hand, and shot Pyrwhit through the heart. I believe the case is mentioned in some of the text-books on homicidal mania.

THE MAGNET

[Subsequent to the inquest on the body of the Rev. Ingram Shallow, who shot himself in the churchyard of St. John's, Ilworthy, Bedfordshire, on the evening of October 14, the following paper was found at his lodgings in the village, and is here published for the first time. It will be remembered that at the inquest the usual verdict of temporary insanity was returned.]

Thursday, October 6.—The world is still ringing with the news of the ghastly accident to the express the night before last. The *Times* has a column and a half. Nothing else is spoken of in the village. Yesterday afternoon I went over on my bicycle to witness the scene of the accident. Of course, the more horrible traces of it had already been removed; the screams of the injured and dying and the sight of mangled bodies, about which we read in the papers, would have been too much for me. The up line was already clear, and it was expected the down line would also be clear in the course of a couple of hours. There was a perfect army of men at work, with every kind of ingenious contrivance for removing the heavy obstacles. All along the embankment fragments of the débris are still strewn. At a distance of at least forty yards from the point where the accident actually happened I found, among some wet grass and fern, a part of one of those plates they have up in the carriages, giving the number that the carriage is intended to carry. I have, often noticed, when standing in the station, the appearance of strength which locomotives and carriages on the fast trains always have. Yet here one saw all this strength of no avail. The engine and the carriages were broken up just like a child's toys. I do most sincerely hope and believe that it was nobody in Ilworthy who was responsible for the disaster. Whoever it is, I do trust and pray that he may be discovered, and that he may pay with his own life for the lives of those hundreds his fiendish action has sent, without a moment of warning, into eternity.

Friday, October 7.—The Vicar came back with me to breakfast this morning after the early service. After some talk about the accident, I asked him if he intended to touch upon it on Sunday morning. He said that he would if I thought it necessary, but that his sermon was already written, being one of a series on the Gospels for the day, which he prepared some time ago. I said that undoubtedly the accident was a terrible event, and one which had sunk very deeply into the minds of everybody in Ilworthy. It was an event which might give point and weight to many a lesson, and it had been my view that Christianity was a practical religion, and the priest should, wherever possible, bring it to bear upon the events of the day. At the same time I did not insist; it was not for me to instruct him, the contrary was rather the case. He smiled good-temperedly, and said that since I seemed to be so full of the accident, and had taken such an absorbing interest in it, I could probably preach a better sermon on it myself, and I might use that as my subject for Sunday evening. I thanked him, and said that I would do so. I have spent the whole day over this sermon. I do not, like the Vicar, read my sermons, but I have written this out in full, and shall commit it to memory. I have given what I think is really a somewhat vivid and impressive picture of the great express rushing at headlong speed to ruin; the obstacle just seen by the driver one moment before his engine crashed into it; the sudden darkness of the train through the extinction of the lights; the screams for help; the sight of the dead bodies laid out on the embankment.... I have worked myself up so much about this sermon that I have only to shut my eyes actually to witness the scene myself. I seem to be standing by the obstruction, and to see the long train crashing down upon me when it is too late to do anything. I hope I am not exciting myself too much about it.

It is already past ten, and I think I shall have a cup of hot cocoa quietly and go to bed. I notice that one of the illustrated papers in the reading-room has a magnificent full-page illustration of the accident. I have often thought, by the way, of writing a little for the papers myself I know I have some taste for the work, and I am inclined to think I have some little gift also. The supplement to one's income would be useful.

Sunday, October 9—I have just returned from church, exhausted. I preached over forty minutes, without the least sign of impatience from any of the congregation. No coughing or shuffling of the feet, or anything of the kind. In the vestry afterwards, Mr. Johnson, our senior churchwarden, took me aside, and told me that it was one of the strongest and most impressive addresses he had ever heard delivered from that pulpit. I hope I did not appear to be unduly pleased at this; one must not think of self in these matters, and I strive against it. I was a little surprised that after this special effort of mine the Vicar should have said nothing at all. He is not a small-minded man, and I cannot believe him to be actuated by jealousy. He spoke of the accident again, and said in what seemed to be rather a patronizing way that he was afraid I was letting it prey too much on my mind. I tried to be humble, and I think I can submit to a rebuke when it is deserved. But, really, this is nonsense. I still picture to myself at times the man standing by the obstruction and watching the express coming towards him. But for the awful wickedness of it, it would be, in a way, a magnificent moment. He would have the thought that he, a weak man, could at his will check the rush of a train, hurl it over, twist and break the strong iron as if it were cardboard, and avenge himself on hundreds of people; and then have all the police in the country hunting for him—and in vain. Exhausted though I am, I am afraid that I shall get no sleep tonight until I have been out in the fresh air a little. The church was crowded, and oppressively hot. The whole village is asleep, and no one will be any the wiser. I think I will get on my bicycle and ride down again to the place where the accident happened. It is within a quarter of an hour to midnight, and so Sunday is practically over. Besides, there are many very good men who do not consider that cycling on Sunday is wrong.

Monday, October 10.—Today I have been beset by a terrible and most extraordinary temptation. I thank God that I have wrestled against it successfully; but the fact that such a temptation could even occur to me appals me.

Tuesday, October 11.—The Vicar called this morning. He will take both sermons next Sunday. He said that I looked ill, and that he thought I had been overdoing it, and was in want of a holiday. I think he is right. He is really a very kind man. I shall go away next week. Again, all day long, I have been subject to the same diabolical impulse. I was half tempted to speak to the Vicar about it, but shame prevented me. I get but little sleep now at nights, and if I do sleep I am always haunted by the same dream. I see the lights of the express coming nearer and nearer....

Wednesday, October 12.—It is done now. It had to be done, and it was no good to contend against it. I believe that it must have been the will of God that I should do it, for ever since the burden has been lifted from my mind, and I have been quite myself again. Late last night, or rather very early this morning, finding myself unable to sleep, I got up and went out. I did not take my bicycle. I ran all the way to that point on the line that I have always been thinking about. There is a stack of heavy sleepers there. It is at the bottom of a deep cutting, and you can see the train coming for some distance. I knew by the tables that I had not much time to spare. I had got six of the heavy sleepers across the rails, when I thought I heard it coming, but I was mistaken. I dragged on another, and then I heard the roar; there was no mistake about it. I could see the lights flashing as I saw them in my dream. I am ashamed that I had not the strength of mind to wait until the last moment. I tried to, but I could not.

I ran away up the embankment and crossed some fields. I saw some men coming and hid behind a hedge. I knew that detectives were about. I lay there panting, and was afraid they would hear me, but they passed on. I got back to my lodgings while it was still dark; nobody had heard me go out, and nobody heard me come back. That is all right.

Since writing the above I have been to the Wednesday evening service. The Vicar was to deliver an address. At the last moment I felt that I wished to preach on this awful accident and the lessons it must have for every one of us. I crossed over to the Vicar and asked permission to preach. He refused. I warned him that I intended to preach, and that if he attempted to occupy the pulpit he would do so at his peril. Then I suddenly seemed to see the matter in a different light and apologized to him. However, I wish very much to address the village on the subject, and as I am not allowed to preach in church I shall call a public meeting on the recreation-ground. I must remember to get arrangements made as to the printing and posting of bills to-morrow.

THE GREEN LIGHT

The man looked down at the figure of the woman on the couch. The little silver clock on the mantelpiece began to chime; he could not bear the sound of it. He flew at the clock like a madman, and dashed it on the ground, and stamped on it. Then he drew down the blind, and opened the door and listened; there was no one on the staircase. Silence seemed now as intolerable to him as sound had been a moment before. He tried to whistle, but his lips were too dry and made only a ridiculous hissing sound. Closing the door behind him, he ran down the staircase and out into the street. The woman on the couch never moved or spoke. It was late in the afternoon; the light from the low sun penetrated the green blind and took from it a horrible colour that seemed to tint the face of the woman on the couch. Flies came out of the dark corners of the room, sulkily busy, crawling and buzzing. One very little fly passed backwards and forwards over the woman's white ringed hand; it moved rapidly, a black speck.

Outside in the street, the man stepped from the pavement into the roadway; a cabman shouted and swore at him, and someone dragged him back by the arm, and told him roughly to look where he was going. He stood still for a minute, and rubbed his forehead with his hand. This would not do. The critical moment had come, the moment when, above all things, it was necessary that his nerve should be perfect and his thoughts clear; and now, when he tried to think, a picture came before the thought and filled his mind—the picture of the white face with the green light upon it. And his heart was beating too fast, and, it seemed to him, almost audibly. He began to feel his pulse, counting the strokes out loud as he stood on the kerb; then he was conscious that two or three boys and loafers were standing in a little group watching him and laughing at him. One of the loafers handed him his hat; it had fallen off when he dodged back on to the pavement, and he had not noticed it. He took the hat, and felt for some coins to give the man. He found a half-crown and a half-penny; he held them in his hand, and stared at them, and forgot why he had wanted them. Then he suddenly remembered and gave them. There was a loud yell of laughter; the boys and loafers were running away, and he heard one of them shouting, 'Let the old stinker out a bit too soon, ain't they?' and another, 'Garn! 'E's tight—that's all's wrong with 'im.'

Again he told himself that this would not do. He must not think of the past—the awful past. He must not think of the future—of his schemes for escape. He must concentrate his thoughts on the present moment, until he could get to some place where he could be alone. Yes, Regent's Park would do well, and it was near. He brushed his hat with his coat-sleeve, put it on, and walked. He thought about the movement of his feet, and the best way to cross the road, and how to avoid running into people, and how to behave as other people in the street behaved. All the things that one generally does unconsciously and automatically required now for their conduct a distinct mental effort.

As he walked on, his mind seemed to clear a little. He reached a spot in Regent's Park where he could lie down in the grass with no one near him, out of sight. 'Now,' he said to himself, 'I need concentrate my thoughts no longer—I can let them go.' In a second he had gone rapidly through the past—the jealousy that had burned in his heart, and the way that he had quieted himself and made his scheme, and carried it out slowly. It had been finished that afternoon, when he had lost control over himself, and—

Through the transparent leaves of the tree near him the sun came with a greenish glare. He shuddered and turned away, so that he could not see it.

Yes, he was to escape—he had made all the arrangements for that. He drew from his side-pocket a roll of notes, and counted them, and entered the numbers in his pocket-book. He had changed a cheque for fifty pounds at the bank that morning. The police would find that out, and endeavour to trace him by discovering where the notes with those numbers were changed. That was one of his means of escape. He would see to it that the notes were never changed by himself, or in any town where he had been or was likely to be. He was going to sacrifice those ten bank-notes to put the police on a wrong scent. He had plenty of money ready in gold—in gold that could not be traced—for his own needs. He chuckled to himself. It was brilliant, this scheme for providing a wrong scent, for making the very carefulness and astuteness of the detectives the stumbling-block in their way; and it would be so easy to get the notes changed by others—the dishonesty of ordinary human beings would serve his purpose.

His mood had changed now to one of exultation. He told himself time after time that he was right. The law would condemn him, but morally he was right, and had only punished the woman as she deserved to be punished. Only, he must escape. And—yes—he must not forget.

He looked round. There was still no one near; but his position did not satisfy him. Not a person must see what he was going to do next. He went on, and found a spot near the canal, where he seemed to be out of sight, and more secure from interruption. Then he took from his pocket a little looking-glass and a pair of scissors. Very carefully he cut away his beard and moustache, that hid the thin-lipped, wide mouth, and the small weak chin. He cut as close as he could, and when he had finished he looked like a man who had neglected to shave for a day or two. A barber would shave him now without suspicion. He was satisfied with the operation. The glass showed him a face so changed that it startled him to look at it. He glanced at his watch—it was time to start for the station, where his luggage had been waiting since the day before, if he meant to get shaved on the way there.

He walked a little way, and sat down again. 'How well everything has been thought out!' he said to himself. All would succeed. With a new name, and in another country, without that drunken, faithless, beautiful woman, he would grow happy again. He had only meant to sit down for a minute or two, but his thoughts rambled and became nonsense, and suddenly he fell into a deep sleep. He had been overtaxed.

An hour passed. The train that he had intended to take steamed out of the station, and still he slept. It grew dusk, and still he slept. When the park-keeper touched him on the shoulder, he half woke, and spoke querulously. Then consciousness came back, and slowly he realized what had happened.

As he walked slowly out of the park, his mind refreshed with sleep, he for the first time realized something else. In the awful moment when he had left the woman, he had broken down, and forgotten everything. The bag of gold was still lying on the table of the room with the green blind. He must go back and get it. It would be horrible to re-enter that room, but it could not be helped. He dared not change the notes himself, and in any case that amount would be insufficient. He must have the gold.

It added, he told himself, slightly to the risk of discovery, but only slightly. His servants had all been sent out and were not to return until half-past nine. No one else could have entered the house. He would find everything as he left it—the gold on the table and the figure of the woman on the couch. He would let himself in with his latch-key. No passer-by would take any notice of so ordinary an incident. He had no occasion to hurry now, and he turned into the first barber's shop that he saw. His mind was as alert now as it had been when he first formed his scheme.

'Let me have your best razor,' he said; 'my skin's tender; in fact, for the last two or three days I haven't been able to shave at all.'

He chatted with the barber about horse-racing, and said that he himself had a couple of horses in training. Then he inquired the way to Piccadilly, saying that he was a stranger in London, and seemed to take careful note of the barber's directions.

He walked briskly away from the shop towards his own house. A comfortable-looking, ruddy-faced woman was coming towards him. A shaft of green light from a chemist's shop-window fell full on her face as she passed, and the horror came back upon him. It was with difficulty that he checked himself from crying out. He hurried on, but that hideous light seemed to linger in his eyes and to haunt him.

'Keep quiet!' he kept saying to himself under his breath. 'Steady yourself; don't be a fool!'

There was an Italian restaurant near, and he went in and drank a couple of glasses of cognac. Then only was he able to go on.

As he turned the corner where his house came into sight he looked up. All the house was dark but for one great green eye in the centre that looked at him. There were lights in that room.

He stood still close to a lamp-post, just touching it to keep his balance. He spoke to himself aloud:

'It's green ... it's green ... someone's there!'

A working man passed him, heard him mumbling, looked at him curiously, and went on.

The great green eye stared at him and fascinated him. Then other lights darted about, red lights, white lights. Someone must be going up and down the staircase and passages. Had she got off the couch? Was the dead woman walking? How his head throbbed! here were two nerves that seemed to sound like two consecutive notes on a piano, struck in slow alternation, then quickening to a rapid shake—whirr! whirr! Now the two notes were struck together, a repeated discord, thumped out—clatter! clatter! No, the sound was outside in the street, and it was the sound of people running. There were boys with excited eyes and white faces, and blowsy, laughing women, and a little old ferret-faced man who coughed as he ran. A police-whistle screamed.

In front of the door of the house a black mass grew up, getting quickly bigger and bigger. It was a crowd of people swaying backwards and forwards, kept back by the police.

The police! He was discovered, then. He must get away at once, not wait another moment. Only the green light was looking at him.

'Stop that light!' he called.

No one noticed him. The green light went on glimmering, and drew him nearer. He had to get there. He was on the outskirts of the crowd now.

Why would not the crowd let him pass? Could not they hear that he was being called? He pushed his way, struggling, dragging people on one side. There were angry voices, a hum growing louder and louder. He caught a woman by the neck and flung her aside. She screamed. Someone struck him in the face, and he tried to strike back. Down! He was down on the road. The air was stifling and stinking there. He tried to get up, and was forced back. Ah! now he was up again, his coat torn off his back, muddy, bleeding, fighting, spitting, howling like a madman.

'Damn you! damn you all!'

The crowd was a storm all round him, tossing him here and there. Again and again he was struck. There was blood streaming over his eyes, and through the blood and mingled with blood he saw the green light looking.

There came a sudden lull. A couple of policemen stood by him, and one of them had him by the arm, and asked him what he was doing. He began to cry, sobbing like a child.

'Take me up there,' he said, panting, 'where the green light is; it's the dead woman calling.'

The policeman stood for a moment hesitating. For a moment the crowd was motionless and silent. Then one of those white-faced boys shrank further back whispering:

'It's the man!'

THE MOON-SLAVE

The Princess Viola had, even in her childhood, an inevitable submission to the dance; a rhythmical madness in her blood answered hotly to the dance music, swaying her, as the wind sways trees, to movements of perfect sympathy and grace.

For the rest, she had her beauty and her long hair, that reached to her knees, and was thought lovable; but she was never very fervent and vivid unless she was dancing; at other times there almost seemed to be a touch of lethargy upon her. Now, when she was sixteen years old, she was betrothed to the Prince Hugo. With others the betrothal was merely a question of state. With her it was merely a question of obedience to the wishes of authority; it had been arranged; Hugo was *comme ci, comme ça*—no god in her eyes; it did not matter. But with Hugo it was quite different—he loved her.

The betrothal was celebrated by a banquet, and afterwards by a dance in the great hall of the palace. From this dance the Princess soon made her escape, quite discontented, and went to the furthest part of the palace gardens, where she could no longer hear the music calling her.

'They are all right,' she said to herself as she thought of the men she had left, 'but they cannot dance. Mechanically they are all right; they have learned it and don't make childish mistakes; but they are only one-two-three machines. They haven't the inspiration of dancing. It is so different when I dance alone.'

She wandered on until she reached an old forsaken maze. It had been planned by a former king. All round it was a high crumbling wall with foxgloves growing on it. The maze itself had all its paths bordered with high opaque hedges; in the very centre was a circular open space with tall pine-trees growing round it. Many years ago the clue to the maze had been lost; it was but rarely now that anyone entered it. Its gravel paths were green with weeds, and in some places the hedges, spreading beyond their borders, had made the way almost impassable.

For a moment or two Viola stood peering in at the gate—a narrow gate with curiously twisted bars of wrought iron surmounted by a heraldic device. Then the whim seized her to enter the maze and try to find the space in the centre. She opened the gate and went in.

Outside everything was uncannily visible in the light of the full moon, but here in the dark shaded alleys the night was conscious of itself. She soon forgot her purpose, and wandered about quite aimlessly, sometimes forcing her way where the brambles had flung a laced barrier across her path, and a dragging mass of convolvulus struck wet and cool upon her cheek. As chance would have it she suddenly found herself standing under the tall pines, and looking at the open space that formed the goal of the maze. She was pleased that she had got there. Here the ground was carpeted with sand, fine and, as it seemed, beaten hard. From the summer night sky immediately above, the moonlight, unobstructed here, streamed straight down upon the scene.

Viola began to think about dancing. Over the dry, smooth sand her little satin shoes moved easily, stepping and gliding, circling and stepping, as she hummed the tune to which they moved. In the centre of the space she paused, looked at the wall of dark trees all round, at the shining stretches of silvery sand and at the moon above.

'My beautiful, moonlit, lonely, old dancing-room, why did I never find you before?' she cried; 'but,' she added, 'you need music—there must be music here.'

In her fantastic mood she stretched her soft, clasped hands upwards towards the moon.

'Sweet moon,' she said in a kind of mock prayer, 'make your white light come down in music into my dancing-room here, and I will dance most deliciously for you to see.' She flung her head backward and let her hands fall; her eyes were half closed, and her mouth was a kissing mouth. 'Ah! sweet moon,' she whispered, 'do this for me, and I will be your slave; I will be what you will.'

Quite suddenly the air was filled with the sound of a grand invisible orchestra. Viola did not stop to wonder. To the music of a slow saraband she swayed and postured. In the music there was the regular beat of small drums and a perpetual drone. The air seemed to be filled with the perfume of some bitter spice. Viola could fancy almost that she saw a smouldering camp-fire and heard far off the roar of some desolate wild beast. She let her long hair fall, raising the heavy strands of it in either hand as she moved slowly to the laden music. Slowly her body swayed with drowsy grace, slowly her satin shoes slid over the silver sand.

The music ceased with a clash of cymbals. Viola rubbed her eyes. She fastened her hair up carefully again. Suddenly she looked up, almost imperiously.

'Music! more music!' she cried.

Once more the music came. This time it was a dance of caprice, pelting along over the violin-strings, leaping, laughing, wanton. Again an illusion seemed to cross her eyes. An old king was watching her, a king with the sordid history of the exhaustion of pleasure written on his flaccid face. A hook-nosed courtier by his side settled the ruffles at his wrists and mumbled, 'Ravissant! Quel malheur que la vieillesse!' It was a strange illusion. Faster and faster she sped to the music, stepping, spinning, pirouetting; the dance was light as thistle-down, fierce as fire, smooth as a rapid stream.

The moment that the music ceased Viola became horribly afraid. She turned and fled away from the moonlit space, through the trees, down the dark alleys of the maze, not heeding in the least which turn she took, and yet she found herself soon at the outside iron gate. From thence she ran through the palace garden, hardly ever pausing to take breath, until she reached the palace itself. In the eastern sky the first signs of dawn were showing; in the palace the festivities were drawing to an end. As she stood alone in the outer hall Prince Hugo came towards her.

'Where have you been, Viola?' he said sternly. 'What have you been doing?'

She stamped her little foot.

'I will not be questioned,' she replied angrily.

'I have some right to question,' he said.

She laughed a little.

'For the first time in my life,' she said, 'I have been dancing.'

He turned away in hopeless silence.

* * * *

The months passed away. Slowly a great fear came over Viola, a fear that would hardly ever leave her. For every month at the full moon, whether she would or no, she found herself driven to the maze, through its mysterious walks into that strange dancing-room. And when she was there the music began once more, and once more she danced most deliciously for the moon to see. The second time that this happened she had merely thought that it was a recurrence of her own whim, and that the music was but a trick that the imagination had chosen to repeat. The third time frightened her, and she knew that the force that sways the tides had strange power over her. The fear grew as the year fell, for each month the music went on for a longer time—each month some of the pleasure had gone from the dance. On bitter nights in winter the moon called her and she came, when the breath was vapour, and the trees that circled her dancing-room were black bare skeletons, and the frost was cruel. She dared not tell anyone, and yet it was with difficulty that she kept her secret. Somehow chance seemed to favour her, and she always found a way to return from her midnight dance to her own room without being observed. Each month the summons seemed to be more imperious and urgent. Once when she was alone on her knees before the lighted altar in the private chapel of the palace she suddenly felt that the words of the familiar Latin prayer had gone from her memory. She rose to her feet, she sobbed bitterly, but the call had come and she could not resist it. She passed out of the chapel and down the palace-gardens. How madly she danced that night!

She was to be married in the spring. She began to be more gentle with Hugo now. She had a blind hope that when they were married she might be able to tell him about it, and he might be able to protect her, for she had always known him to be fearless. She could not love him, but she tried to be good to him. One day he mentioned to her that he had tried to find his way to the centre of the maze, and had failed. She smiled faintly. If only she could fail! But she never did.

On the night before the wedding, day she had gone to bed and slept peacefully, thinking with her last waking moments of Hugo. Overhead the full moon came up the sky. Quite suddenly Viola was wakened with the impulse to fly to the dancing-room. It seemed to bid her hasten with breathless speed. She flung a cloak around her, slipped her naked feet into her dancing-shoes, and hurried forth. No one saw her or heard her—on the marble staircase of the palace, on down the terraces of the garden, she ran as fast as she could. A thorn-plant caught in her cloak, but she sped on, tearing it free; a sharp stone cut through the satin of one shoe, and her foot was wounded and bleeding, but she sped on. As the pebble that is flung from the cliff must fall until it reaches the sea, as the white ghost-moth must come in from cool hedges and scented darkness to a burning death in the lamp by which you sit so late—so Viola had no choice. The moon called her. The moon drew her to that circle of hard, bright sand and the pitiless music.

It was brilliant, rapid music to-night. Viola threw off her cloak and danced. As she did so, she saw that a shadow lay over a fragment of the moon's edge. It was the night of a total eclipse. She heeded it not. The intoxication of the dance was on her. She was all in white; even her face was pale in the moonlight. Every movement was full of poetry and grace.

The music would not stop. She had grown deathly weary. It seemed to her that she had been dancing for hours, and the shadow had nearly covered the moon's face, so that it was almost dark. She could hardly see the trees around her. She went on dancing, stepping, spinning, pirouetting, held by the merciless music.

It stopped at last, just when the shadow had quite covered the moon's face, and all was dark. But it stopped only for a moment, and then began again. This time it was a slow, passionate waltz. It was useless to resist; she began to dance once more. As she did so she uttered a sudden shrill scream of horror, for in the dead darkness a hot hand had caught her own and whirled her round, *and she was no longer dancing alone.*

* * * *

The search for the missing Princess lasted during the whole of the following day. In the evening Prince Hugo, his face anxious and firmly set, passed in his search the iron gate of the maze, and noticed on the stones beside it the stain of a drop of blood. Within the gate was another stain. He followed this clue, which had been left by Viola's wounded foot, until he reached that open space in the centre that had served Viola for her dancing-room. It was quite empty. He noticed that the sand round the edges was all worn down, as though someone had danced there, round and round, for a long time. But no separate footprint was distinguishable there. Just outside this track, however, he saw two footprints clearly defined close together: one was the print of a tiny satin shoe; the other was the print of a large naked foot—a cloven foot.

THIS IS ALL

It was a very hot summer day. The doctor's brougham had been waiting in the shade of the chestnut avenue leading to the big white house. Then a servant brought out a message.

'Morning, Jameson'—he knew the coachman. 'Stopping to luncheon—you're to go round to the stables.'

'I guessed as much. What—is he worse this morning?'

'No, not a bit of it.' Then, confidentially: 'Between ourselves, there's no more the matter with Mr. Wyatt nor there is with you nor me.'

'So I've always supposed.' If you can be surprised at anything you will not make a good coachman. 'Well—see you again later.' And the wheels crunched slowly along the gravel.

In the meantime Mr. Alexander Wyatt paced the entire length of his great library. He was lean, tall, bent in the shoulders. His hair was gray and rather too long; his face was clean-shaven and ashy in colour. He looked worried—hunted.

Dr. Holling watched him narrowly. The doctor was no younger, but his hair was black. He was a giant—his chest was broad and deep, and he stood six foot three in his socks. His face was slightly florid, and his figure showed some tendency towards corpulence. But he looked like a man of the world, and not like a mere sensualist—there was that distinction. Under the heavy brows were the eyes of a man who knows what he wants to know and is quite sure that he knows it. He looked confident and clever.

'My dear fellow,' said the doctor, 'the long and short of it is that you ought to have come to me long ago. I don't mean in Harley Street—I mean here at home. Of course, I wouldn't see any ordinary patient here; but an old friend like you—yes, really you ought to have come to me.'

'I might have gone up to Harley Street. It's only an hour away. You go there and back most days in the year, and I might have taken the journey for once. I don't know why I didn't—I had thought of it—but you're always so busy.'

'Busy? Well, yes. But I don't let myself be so busy that I can't see a friend who's ill.'

Wyatt sighed heavily.

'And now you're spoiling one of your rare holidays for my sake. I say, old man, do take a fee—a proper fee—something in proportion.'

'Now, don't talk like that. If fees had had anything to do with it, could I have come to you and suggested that it might be as well if I just went over you? Besides, I wouldn't give up a day of my holiday for any fee. Why should I? I've already made more money than I shall ever spend. I'm not stopping because I've got a patient. I'm stopping because an old friend is ill.'

'It's very good of you—very, very good.'

'Come back to the point. Why didn't you send for me before—you must have known that you were ill?'

'I had my suspicions. I—I didn't want to think about it.'

'And so you waited until, from mere casual observation, I also had my suspicions, and told you so. I think you were foolish. Come now: what were you afraid of? I haven't hurt you.'

'No, no,' said Wyatt. 'Of course not. But I didn't want to know that I was going to die.' There was a longish pause, and Wyatt's eyes grew rounder and stared. 'O, my God! O, my God!' he muttered to himself.

'Well?' said Dr. Holling.

He hated these exhibitions, but he spoke sympathetically.

'I can't die!' stammered Wyatt, 'It—it—it mustn't be.'

'You will find ultimately that you can die,' said Dr. Holling. 'We all shall. If you will persist in working yourself up into this condition of shivering cowar—of nervous panic, you will die rather sooner, or possibly very much sooner, than you otherwise would. Come, man, you may have another ten or a dozen years, if you'll avoid every kind of stress. You're wealthy, have no ambitions, have no hard work, are not passionately attached to anybody. It is highly unlikely that the stress will come upon you from the outside—take care that it does not come from yourself.'

'You're right, you're right. I shall pull myself together,' he said; but he still spoke excitedly. 'I—I only gave way for the moment. Ten or a dozen years at the least; with absolute moderation, quiet living, self-restraint, and so on, who knows that it might not be a score of years?'

The doctor looked at him curiously and said nothing.

'There, you see—I'm all right. I've faced the situation. And now tell me exactly what's the matter with me.'

'Heart,' said the doctor laconically.

'I know that,' Wyatt said irritably. 'I want to know the name of the disease, and if there's any complication.'

'Well, I shan't tell you. You'd try to look yourself up in your old edition of Roberts's "Theory and Practice of Medicine," and you'd find something more or less like yourself, and it wouldn't do you any good.'

'Some doctors would have told me.'

'Hang it! then, go and ask them,' said Dr. Holling quite quietly. 'Whomever else I meet in consultation, it's quite certain I won't meet my own patient.'

'Of course not. I only mentioned it. I'm not silly enough to go to any other doctor—never dreamed of it. Of course, I know very well that you're the first man on heart. I'm not so ignorant of medicine as you suppose.'

'Ah!' said the doctor cheerfully, 'I wish you were twice as ignorant, or else knew a thousand times as much as you do.'

Luncheon was announced. The doctor rose smiling. Poor Wyatt did what he could during luncheon to shake off the heavy depression that weighed on him, but he did not make much of a host. He could only talk of his own illness, and speculate on what death really was. On these subjects Dr. Holling had little to say, but he spoke of the rising value of land in the neighbourhood; and Wyatt was a landlord. Wyatt heard with a wretchedly simulated cheerfulness on his sad-eyed, sallow face. What would it profit him though he gained the whole world?

Wyatt had been in his day the brightest and best of companions; but when a man's material heart within him has taken on autumnal tints the man's spirits droop also. Both, the doctor knew, were symptomatic.

And he who knew this, and had known the old Wyatt, was patient; but when he was being driven away from the great white house he became very sad.

* * * *

That afternoon Wyatt sat crouching in a big easy-chair in his library, alone. It was a hot day, but he had a shawl wrapped round his feet: latterly his feet had been always cold, as though already they felt the chill of wet earth. There was a pile of books on the table beside him, and on the floor. He turned avidly and restlessly from one to the other. There were comforting books of religion; there were terrifying books of religion; there were works of metaphysics; there were blasphemous diatribes; there was science conscious of its limitations. Now he would take for company some drunken tinker jeering at the notion of a hereafter, repelling by its brutal ignorance but appealing by its complete self-confidence. And now again he would hear the calm voice of science: 'There are beautiful stories, but I dare not tell you that they are true. In some places, where it has been possible to test them, I have tested and found they were not true. As to the rest, those stories seem more beautiful than probable. I still wait for verification or disproof—not with folded hands, but working at other things.'

He had always feared death, and now for many long days and nights he had busied himself in this futile search for something certain about it. He heard a hundred voices all crying differently, and knew not to which he should listen.

He used to make attempts, from time to time, to pull himself together; he made one now.

'What does all this concern me?' he said aloud. 'I'm not going to die. Holling said so. Holling gave me twenty years, with reasonable care, and he knows what he is talking about.' He pushed the books aside contemptuously. 'Pack of nonsense!' He picked up instead a catalogue that his wine merchant had sent him. There was some port of a fairly recent vintage that he wished to put down. 'That's it,' he said, marking the catalogue with pencil, 'we'll say fifty dozen.' He rubbed his chilly hands together, and hummed a light tune.

At five his man Jackson brought him in a glass of whisky-and-water, carefully measured. Wyatt had got into the habit of drinking a good deal of strong tea in the afternoon while he pottered over his collections—one philatelic, the other eighteenth-century autographs. The doctor had forbidden tea, and Wyatt, even when he was pulling himself together, obeyed the doctor.

Holling had forbidden late hours also. Wyatt had induced—actually induced—the habit of insomnia. Before the doctor's interference he would never go to bed before two or three in the morning. After one of his own delightful dinners, or if he had been dining out, he would still sit up. He professed that these hours were of incalculable value—that he could not live in society unless for a little time each day he lived absolutely alone. All the lights were put out except in the library; the rest of the house went to sleep. Wyatt smoked, read, thought about things. At intervals he sipped strong coffee. It was only when he found himself unable to keep awvake that he lit his candle and went upstairs. Every night, or early morning, as his candle lit the long mirror on the landing, he saw himself reflected, and the reflection always came as a surprise. He never looked as he supposed that he looked; sometimes the reflection seemed almost unrecognisable.

'I can't sleep before three in the morning,' Wyatt had maintained to the doctor.

'Then it must be morphia,' said Holling.

He called that night with a hypodermic syringe, and that night Wyatt went up to bed at ten o'clock and slept at once.

'But I mustn't go on with morphia, of course,' said Wyatt knowingly.

'It won't be necessary,' said Holling. 'You see, after I've given it you for three nights, I shall have broken through your habit. Then you at once return to the normal state, and go to sleep at the ordinary time.'

The doctor reeled off this absolute nonsense with an air of the utmost gravity and conviction. He knew his patient. He had never given him any morphia at all—he had punctured the skin, but injected nothing. Wyatt's insomnia yielded completely to discreet and masterly humbug and the abolition of his after-dinner coffee.

Strong tea and late hours were quite given up now. Wyatt was positively anxious to give things up; in his mad terror of death he had grown to regard it as a monster to be appeased by sacrifice. He had a notion—vague but deeply rooted—that the more he gave up the longer he would live. He was almost disappointed that the doctor did not forbid stimulants.

* * * *

Jackson, Wyatt's servant, had been with him for twenty years. When Wyatt was alone it was Jackson himself who made the after-dinner coffee—for on this point Wyatt mistrusted women. Jackson was a creature of habit. For over a week he had diligently remembered that coffee was forbidden. Tonight he forgot it; habit asserted itself, and twenty minutes after Wyatt had left the dining-room for the library, Jackson entered the library with the coffee. He was considerably startled at his reception.

Fits of deep depression sometimes alternate with fits of extreme irritation. Wyatt flew into a mad rage. He swore the wretched man was trying to kill him, ordered him out of the house, and abused him virulently, loudly, and at length. 'Go, go!' he shrieked finally.

Jackson conveyed the news to the kitchen that there was only one thing the matter with Mr. Wyatt—he was clean off his head, that was all.

As Jackson left the library Wyatt dropped into a chair, his face contorted, covered with sweat, bending forward, his hands tightly fixed against his chest. That awful anginal pain! No, it had never been like that before. It must mean death. Ah, if he could only get to that bell! He tried to call. The words, 'Dr. Holling … at once,' came out in a whisper.

The pain ceased, almost suddenly. A strange calm came over him, and for the first time in many days he thought of other people. Dr. Holling? Of course he would not send for him. It would be too bad, at that time of night—altogether too bad. Besides, it was his own fault. He had given way to temper, and had been punished for it. Why, he might have died. Upon his word, it would have served him right if he *had* died. Poor Jackson! It was the first time in his life he had spoken to Jackson like that. Well, when he came to die Jackson was remembered in his will, and would forgive him. After all, why live so long, at such care, with such trouble? Nature calls—obey cheerfully.

And the calm became drowsiness, and the drowsiness became sleep all very quickly. It was a lovely sleep, with a consciousness of well-being permeating its faintly-sketched dreams.

Jackson looked in at ten o'clock, at a quarter-past, at twenty-five minutes past, and at half-past.

Then he sought Mrs. Palfrey, the housekeeper.

'He's still asleep,' said Jackson.

'You're sure it's sleep?' said Mrs. Palfrey gloomily.

'Oh, I leave to-morrow, anyhow, whatever he says,' said Jackson. 'It's the responsibility I can't stand. It's wearing me. But come and see for yourself.'

They opened the library door cautiously and peered in.

'The top of his shirt-front's moving,' said Mrs. Palfrey in an undertone. 'He's asleep.'

'Don't he look awful? I 'on't wake him. I swear I 'on't wake him.'

'Better not. Put his candle on the table, by the lamp; cough, as if accidental, as you go out. Then if he wakes, so much the better. If not, we'll all go to bed, and you'll put the lights out, same as in the old days.'

Jackson shivered, and followed this advice carefully. The cough (as if accidental) was unavailing, and the lights were put out. Only in the library the lamplight fell on the gleaming shirt-front, still moving. And on the landing the full-length mirror waited, its eyes closed in the darkness, but ready to wake as the lighted candle came slowly up the staircase, and to reflect in a moment the figure of the master of the house, dishevelled, late, on his way to bed.

* * * *

He was awake. The lamp had burned itself out; the dawn, the early midsummer dawn, was already advanced; its light came, tempered yet sufficient, through the ugly Venetian blinds. From the garden and the country beyond came the shrill concert of innumerable birds. A heavy cart jolted and bumped to early work on some distant road. No, there was no need of the candle; he would go to bed by daylight, with that delightful sense of well-being, that firm conviction that there was no good in worry or argument, still comforting him.

Ah! how often at this hour he had trod the stairs, with a fantastic curiosity to see what he looked like in the tall mirror. By this time his head should have appeared in it, coming close to the Japanese cabinet. There in the mirror gleamed the pale gold of the cabinet, and there was the blue-and-white of the tall Oriental vase, and there were the masses of dark shadow beyond. Alexander Wyatt found all there but himself. Him only the mirror gave back no more. Back! back to the library as in a panic. Something has happened!

And there in the library the spirit of Alexander Wyatt, that the mirror saw not, found in the easy-chair the huddled body, dressed in clothes that no longer moved to the breathing.

'I am dead,' said Alexander Wyatt, 'and this—this—this is all.'

THE DIARY OF A GOD

During the week there had been several thunderstorms. It was after the last of these, on a cool Saturday evening, that he was found at the top of the hill by a shepherd. His speech was incoherent and disconnected; he gave his name correctly, but could or would add no account of himself. He was wet through, and sat there pulling a sprig of heather to pieces. The shepherd afterwards said that he had great difficulty in persuading him to come down, and that he talked much nonsense. In the path at the foot of the hill he was recognised by some people from the farmhouse where he was lodging, and was taken back there. They had, indeed, gone out to look for him. He was subsequently removed to an asylum, and died insane a few months later.

* * * *

Two years afterwards, when the furniture of the farmhouse came to be sold by auction, there was found in a little cupboard in the bedroom which he had occupied an ordinary penny exercise-book. This was partly filled, in a beautiful and very regular handwriting, with what seems to have been something in the nature of a diary, and the following are extracts from it:

June 1st.—It is absolutely essential to be quiet. I am beginning life again, and in quite a different way, and on quite a different scale, and I cannot make the break suddenly. I must have a pause of a few weeks in between the two different lives. I saw the advertisement of the lodgings in this farmhouse in an evening paper that somebody had left at the restaurant. That was when I was trying to make the change abruptly, and I may as well make a note of what happened.

After attending the funeral (which seemed to me an act of hypocrisy, as I hardly knew the man, but it was expected of me), I came back to my Charlotte Street rooms and had tea. I slept well that night. Then next morning I went to the office at the usual hour, in my best clothes, and with a deep band still on my hat. I went to Mr. Toller's room and knocked. He said, 'Come in,' and after I had entered: 'Can I do anything for you? What do you want?'

Then I explained to him that I wished to leave at once. He said:

'This seems sudden, after thirty years' service.'

'Yes,' I replied. 'I have served you faithfully for thirty years, but things have changed, and I have now three hundred a year of my own. I will pay something in lieu of notice, if you like, but I cannot go on being a clerk any more. I hope, Mr. Toller, you will not think that I speak with any impertinence to yourself, or any immodesty, but I am really in the position of a private gentleman.'

He looked at me curiously, and as he did not say anything I repeated:

'I think I am in the position of a private gentleman.'

In the end he let me go, and said very politely he was sorry to lose me. I said good-bye to the other clerks, even to those who had sometimes laughed at what they imagined to be my peculiarities. I gave the better of the two office-boys a small present in money.

I went back to the Charlotte Street rooms, but there was nothing to do there. There were figures going on in my head, and my fingers seemed to be running up and down columns. I had a stupid idea that I should be in trouble if Mr. Toller were to come in and catch me like that. I went out and had a capital lunch, and then I went to the theatre. I took a stall right in the front row, and sat there all by myself. Then I had a cab to the restaurant. It was too soon for dinner, so I ordered a whisky-and-soda, and smoked a few cigarettes. The man at the table next me left the evening paper in which I saw the advertisement of these farmhouse lodgings. I read the whole of the paper, but I have forgotten it all except that advertisement, and I could say it by heart now—all about bracing air and perfect quiet and the rest of it. For dinner I had a bottle of champagne. The waiter handed me a list, and asked which I would prefer. I waved the list away and said:

'Give me the best.'

He smiled. He kept on smiling all through dinner until the end; then he looked serious. He kept getting more serious. Then he brought two other men to look at me. They spoke to me, but I did not want to talk. I think I fell asleep. I found myself in my rooms in Charlotte Street next morning, and my landlady gave me notice because, she said, I had come home beastly drunk. Then that advertisement flashed into my mind about the bracing air. I said:

'I should have given you notice in any case; this is not a suitable place for a gentleman.'

June 3rd.—I am rather sorry that I wrote down the above. It seems so degrading. However, it was merely an act of ignorance and carelessness on my part, and, besides, I am writing solely for myself. To myself I may own freely that I made a mistake, that I was not used to the wine, and that I had not fully gauged what the effects would be. The incident is disgusting, but I simply put it behind me, and think no more about it. I pay here two pounds ten shillings a week for my two rooms and board. I take my meals, of course, by myself in the sitting-room. It would be rather cheaper if I took them with the family, but I do not care about that. After all, what is two pounds ten shillings a week? Roughly speaking, a hundred and thirty pounds a year.

June 17th.—I have made no entry in my diary for some days. For a certain period I have had no heart for that or for anything else. I had told the people here that I was a private gentleman (which is strictly true), and that I was engaged in literary pursuits. By the latter I meant to imply no more than that I am fond of reading, and that it is my intention to jot down from time to time my sensations and experiences in the new life which has burst upon me. At the same time I have been greatly depressed. Why, I can hardly explain. I have been furious with myself. Sitting in my own sitting-room, with a gold-tipped cigarette between my fingers, I have been possessed (even though I recognised it as an absurdity) by a feeling that if Mr. Toller were to come in suddenly I should get up and apologize. But the thing which depressed me most was the open country. I have read, of course, those penny stories about the poor little ragged boys who never see the green leaf in their lives, and I always thought them exaggerated. So they are exaggerated: there are the Embankment Gardens with the Press Band playing; there are parks; there are Sunday-school treats. All these little ragged boys see the green leaf, and to say they do not is an exaggeration—I am afraid a wilful exaggeration. But to see the open country is quite a different thing. Yesterday was a fine day, and I was out all day in a place called Wensley Dale. On one spot where I stood I could see for miles all round. There was not a single house, or tree, or human being in sight. There was just myself on the top of a moor; the bigness of it gave me a regular scare. I suppose I had got used to walls: I had got used to feeling that if I went straight ahead without stopping I should knock against something. That somehow made me feel safe. Out on that great moor—just as if I were the last man left alive in the world—I do not feel safe. I find the track and get home again, and I tremble like a half-drowned kitten until I see a wall again, or somebody with a surly face who does not answer civilly when I speak to him. All these feelings will wear off, no doubt, and I shall be able to enter upon the new phase of my existence without any discomfort. But I was quite right to take a few months' quiet retirement. One must get used to things gradually. It was the same with the champagne—to which, by the way, I had not meant to allude any further.

June 20th.—It is remarkable what a fascination these very large moors have for me. It is not exactly fear any more—indeed, it must be the reverse. I do not care to be anywhere else. Instead of making this a mere pause between two different existences, I shall continue it. To that I have quite made up my mind. When I am out there in a place where I cannot see any trees, or houses, or living things, I am the last person left alive in the world. I am a kind of a god. There is nobody to think anything at all about me, and it does not matter if my clothes are not right, or if I drop an 'h'—which I rarely do except when speaking very quickly. I never knew what real independence was before. There have been too many houses around, and too many people looking on. It seems to me now such a common and despicable thing to live among people, and to have one's character and one's ways altered by what they are going to think. I know now that when I ordered that bottle of champagne I did it far more to please the waiter and to make him think well of me than to please myself. I pity the kind of creature that I was then, but I had not known the open country at that time. It is a grand education. If Toller were to come in now I should say, 'Go away. Go back to your bricks and mortar, and account-books, and swell friends, and white waistcoats, and rubbish of that kind. You cannot possibly understand me, and your presence irritates me. If you do not go at once I will have the dog let loose upon you.' By the way, that was a curious thing which happened the other day. I feed the dog, a mastiff, regularly, and it goes out with me. We had walked some way, and had reached that spot where a man becomes the last man alive in the world. Suddenly the dog began to howl, and ran off home with its tail between its legs, as if it were frightened of something. What was it that the dog had seen and I had not seen? A ghost? In broad daylight? Well, if the dead come back they might walk here without contamination. A few sheep, a sweep of heather, a gray sky, but nothing that a living man planted or built. They could be alone here. If it were not that it would seem a kind of blasphemy, I would buy a piece of land in the very middle of the loneliest moor and build myself a cottage there.

June 23rd.—I received a letter today from Julia. Of course she does not understand the change which has taken place in me. She writes as she always used to write, and I find it very hard to remember and realize that I liked it once, and was glad when I got a letter from her. That was before I got into the habit of going into empty places alone. The old clerking, account-book life has become too small to care about. The swell life of the private gentleman, to which I looked forward, is also not worth considering. As for Julia, I was to have married her; I used to kiss her. She wrote to say that she thought a great deal of me; she still writes. I don't want her. I don't want anything. I have become the last man alive in the world. I shall leave this farmhouse very soon. The people are all right, but they are people, and therefore insufferable. I can no longer live or breathe in a place where I see people, or trees which people have planted, or houses which people have built. It is an ugly word—people.

July 7th.—I was wrong in saying that I was the last man alive in the world. I believe I am dead. I know now why the mastiff howled and ran away. The whole moor is full of them; one sees them after a time when one has got used to the open country—or perhaps it is because one is dead. Now I see them by moonlight and sunlight, and I am not frightened at all. I think I must be dead, because there seems to be a line ruled straight through my life, and the things which happened on the further side of the line are not real. I look over this diary, and see some references to a Mr. Toller, and to some champagne, and coming into money. I cannot for the life of me think what it is all about. I suppose the incidents described really happened, unless I was mad when I wrote about them. I suppose that I am not dead, since I can write in a book, and eat food, and walk, and sleep and wake again. But since I see them now—these people that fill up the lonely places—I must be quite different to ordinary human beings. If I am not dead, then what am I? Today I came across an old letter signed 'Julia Jarvis'; the envelope was addressed to me. I wonder who on earth she was?

July 9th.—A man in a frock-coat came to see me, and talked about my best interest. He wanted me, so far as I could gather, to come away with him somewhere. He said I was all right, or, at any rate, would become all right, with a little care. He would not go away until I said that I would kill him. Then the woman at the farmhouse came up with a white face, and I said I would kill her too. I positively cannot endure people. I am something apart, something different. I am not alive, and I am not dead. I cannot imagine what I am.

July 16*th.*—I have settled the whole thing to my complete satisfaction. I can without doubt believe the evidence of my own senses. I have seen, and I have heard. I know now that I am a god. I had almost thought before that this might be. What was the matter was that I was too diffident: I had no self-confidence; I had never heard before of any man, even a clerk in an old-established firm, who had become a god. I therefore supposed it was impossible until it was distinctly proved to be.

I had often made up my mind to go to that range of hills that lies to the north. They are purple when one sees them far off. At nearer view they are gray, then they become green, then one sees a silver network over the green. The silver network is made by streams descending in the sunlight. I climbed the hill slowly; the air was still, and the heat was terrible. Even the water which I drank from the running stream seemed flat and warm. As I climbed, the storm broke. I took but little notice of it, for the dead that I had met below on the moor had told me that lightning could not touch me. At the top of the hill I turned, and saw the storm raging beneath my feet. It is the greatest of mercies that I went there, for that is where the other gods gather, at such times as the lightning plays between them and the earth, and the black thunder-clouds, hanging low, shut them out from the sight of men.

Some of the gods were rather like the big pictures that I have seen on the hoardings, advertising plays at the theatre, or some food which is supposed to give great strength and muscular development. They were handsome in face, and without any expression. They never seemed to be angry or pleased, or hurt. They sat there in great long rows, resting, with the storm raging in between them and the earth. One of them was a woman. I spoke to her, and she told me that she was older than this earth; yet she had the face of a young girl, and her eyes were like eyes that I have seen before some-where. I cannot think where I saw the eyes like those of the goddess, but perhaps it was in that part of my life which is forgotten and ruled off with a line. It gave one the greatest and most majestic feelings to stand there with the gods, and to know that one was a god one's self, and that lightning did not hurt one, and that one would live for ever.

July 18*th.*—This afternoon the storm returned, and I hurried to the meeting-place, but it is far away to the hills, and though I climbed as quickly as I could the storm was almost passed, and they had gone.

August 1*st.*—I was told in my sleep that tomorrow I was to go back to the hill again, and that once more the gods would be there, and that the storm would gather round us, and would shut us from profane sight, and the steely lightnings would blind any eye that tried to look upon us. For this reason I have refused now to eat or drink anything; I am a god and have no need of such things. It is strange that now when I see all real things so clearly and easily—the ghosts of the dead that walk across the moors in the sunlight and the concourse of the gods on the hill-top above the storm—men and women with whom I once moved before I became a god are no more to me than so many black shadows. I scarcely know one from the other, only that the presence of a black shadow anywhere near me makes me angry, and I desire to kill it. That will pass away; it is probably some faint relic of the thing that I once was in the other side of my life on the other side of the line which has been ruled across it. Seeing that I am a god it is not natural that I can feel anger or joy any more. Already all feeling of joy has gone from me, for to-morrow, so I was told in my sleep, I am to be betrothed to the beautiful goddess that is older than the world, and yet looks like a young girl, and she is to give me a sprig of heather as a token and—

* * * *

It was on the evening of August 1 he was found.